Secrets Among Us

Granite Peak Security

KARICE BOLTON

SECRETS AMONG US

Chapter One

Sadie

"I would be lying if I didn't tell you I'm going to miss you," Melanie said, shaking her head.

I pushed my lips into a forced smile and nodded. "I'm going to miss you like crazy, but it's for the best. I need to go back home to my family in New Hampshire."

Melanie leaned against the counter of the coffee shop I'd called home for the last six months and sighed. She'd become one of my closest friends in Washington since I moved here. The moment I met her, it felt like I'd known her forever. There was just something so familiar about her, and it reminded me of back home.

"I know. I get it. I still can't believe you left everything you knew back east. That's extremely brave, and I don't have that in me." She shivered. "Even moving here and buying this place were a big deal for me."

"You've done fabulously with everything, and you are a risk-taker. Buying this place from the previous owners was a big deal."

She shook her head. "No. I don't take risks. It's why I bought this coffee shop. I knew it was already successful. I'm more of a wash, rinse, repeat type of gal. Anything new makes me break out in hives."

"Should I get that on a T-shirt for you?" I asked, chuckling and pulling my dark blonde hair into a quick ponytail.

The truth was that I wasn't brave at all. I was the exact opposite of brave. I was running from a nightmare that seemed to follow me everywhere and destroy anything that created happiness.

Zack Parker's words floated through my mind, and I blinked the sadness away.

I'll protect you so that you can stop running.

And then I remembered my reply.

I can't run away from my mind, Zack. And that's my problem and shouldn't be yours.

Breaking up with him was for the best. We shared a traumatic history, and it wasn't healthy.

It just wasn't.

My throat clenched at my last thought, and I sipped the very last pumpkin spice latte I'd made for myself at Granite Beans.

I didn't need to become another cliché. I already felt out of my element with everything that had happened to me, and falling in love with my rescuer wasn't a good idea.

Even if it had already happened.

The truth was that I loved it out here in Washington. Being nestled in a mountain town where tourists only visited on the weekends left the weekdays for the locals to do a lot of quiet contemplating, and that was what I'd needed… until recently.

Now, it felt like my thoughts were suffocating me, and all eyes were on me. I'd be at the grocery store and get a creeping sensation up my spine. I'd go to pick up a hamburger at the local hangout and feel like someone was lurking in a booth, watching me. It had started the week before I'd ended things with my boyfriend.

Of course, I'd see nothing whenever I turned around to check things out.

Nothing.

My eyes met Melanie's. "Well, you can come visit anytime. But I'd probably wait until after I'm out of my parents' house, or it will feel like a slumber party from your teens." I shook my head. "That is the one thing that's hard to swallow. I'm headed into my thirties and moving back in with Mom and Dad."

"Oh, please. They're going to love having you." She grinned and shook her head, letting her red hair cascade past her shoulders. "You promise you'll let me haunt you in New England when you're all settled?"

"Promise." I nodded, thinking about the encroaching fall weather. I'd always loved this time of year when leaves were changing and a crispness nipped at my nose.

So much had happened to me in the last six months that it was hard to focus on what I wanted, but I knew there was nothing left for me out here but heartache.

I'd made a decision, and I needed to stick with it.

At least back in New Hampshire, I could wallow around a little about my breakup and have my sister and parents pick me back up.

"What did Zack say about the move?" she asked, knowing enough about our relationship to not be worrisome but enough to ask the hard questions.

That was why it was nice to have coworkers as friends. I could feel social but keep everyone at a distance.

In fact, she knew very little about my past at all. I'd tried to keep it that way but still felt close to Melanie.

"I haven't told him yet. I might not." I shrugged. "At least until I move."

Her brows rose, and she made a clicking sound with her tongue. "I see. So basically, you'll make me do the hard part when he comes in one morning for his large Americano and asks where you're at?"

I giggled and eyed her over the rim of my cup. "Maybe."

"Will you do one thing for me?" she asked softly, walking over to me. "Let me hug you?"

I groaned but stopped myself from recoiling. I'd been working on it with my online therapist for months. But with everything I'd gone through, it was safe to say that I was no longer a hugger.

"Sure," I said through gritted teeth as she dove in for a squeeze, utterly oblivious that I was as stiff as a board, but that was why I adored Melanie.

She had a quirky oblivion that I craved for my sanity, but instead, I was left with a mind that wouldn't turn off.

"See? It's not so bad," she mumbled as she hugged me harder.

Her arms felt like a strap tightening that I couldn't break free from. I clenched my eyes shut and took a deep breath, slowly exhaling as she stepped back.

Melanie studied me and quickly dropped her arms to her sides. "I'm sorry. I didn't know…"

I chuckled, trying to make it less awkward, but it wasn't working. "It's not you. It's me. Totally me."

Her brow quirked. "Usually, it's some guy with a beard who's telling me that."

I snickered. "I'm going to miss you, Mel. You always know the perfect thing to say."

"Are you sure there's nothing I can do to make you stay? Like promise to clean your apartment for a year or give you free coffee?"

"You already give me free coffee." I winked at her. "But, no. I need to go back home. It's too hard to be in this town when Zack's here, and I know I can't make things work with him, and I need family right now."

She let out a deep breath. "I know, and I fully support you. I just don't know how Zack is going to take it. He hasn't been the same when he comes in for his usual."

Hearing that tugged at my heart.

"He'll be fine. He's strong and stable, a total

catch. He'll find someone soon, and the quicker I'm out of his hair, the better." It was as if I lied to myself enough times, it would come true.

A faint smile touched her lips. "Are you sure you don't want to tell him?"

I shook my head, but her eyes filled with surprise as her gaze darted over my shoulders.

And then I heard the sound.

The one voice that could ignite every part of my body was right behind me.

"Tell me what?" The gruffness of his tone made my heart break a little more.

He was supposed to be in Alaska this week.

This entire week.

That was one of the many reasons I chose to go back home. He was rarely here anyway.

Melanie's eyes widened while she grabbed an empty cup, filled it with coffee, and handed it to Zack.

"I'll be in the back organizing syrups or napkins or rubber bands." She pressed her lips together, looked at the both of us, and spun around.

I closed my eyes before facing him and tried to

get my bearings.

"Aren't you supposed to be in Alaska?" My arms folded over my chest, and I spun around, blinking my eyes open to see the one and only man I'd ever fallen in love with.

Zack's gaze connected with mine, and an impossible charge of longing drifted through me. "What aren't you planning on telling me, Sadie?"

He stepped forward, put his coffee on the counter, and propped an elbow on the large piece of granite as he watched me. I felt the instant pull I always had from the moment his arms slid around me and he scooped me into him, carrying me to safety so many months ago.

This was the problem with Zack.

He could read my mind like nobody else.

The man knew when I was hurting.

Zack knew when I wanted to run.

When I was scared.

When I was having nightmares.

He knew me better than myself.

But every single time I looked at him, my mind

flashed to the day he saved my life.

The day I thought was my last.

I bit my lip and pushed myself away from the counter, grabbing my empty mug as I walked to the coffee machine to pour a cup of coffee.

"Sadie, what's going on?" The urgency in his voice was like a million little stabs to my heart. "What aren't you telling me?"

I took a sip of the coffee, willing myself not to cry.

"It's just that..." I took a deep breath and set my coffee down, but no words would come.

His eyes caught mine. "It's just that...?" His voice softened, opening the door to my confession.

"I'm going back home."

His entire body stiffened, and panic set in his gaze as he shook his head. "That's not a good idea."

I scowled and picked up my cup again.

I rarely liked being told what was and wasn't a good idea. That was how I wound up in Washington in the first place. My family was ultimately against the idea. Well, most of my family. My sister fully supported me, and it seemed like a good idea at the time.

"It's the best idea I've got, Zack. It's unhealthy for me to wander around a small town like this with an ex I could bump into at any second."

"I'm rarely here," he argued.

"Duly noted," I muttered under my breath.

"That's not fair." He shook his head, sliding his fingers through the dark strands.

It was always these little things he did that drove me insane for him. The way his dark, wavy hair curled around his fingers or the small dimple that would surface on his left cheek when he smirked, but not when he smiled. Or the intensity in his hazel eyes that turned me into a zombie as I watched the clarity behind his gaze grow.

"You know what I do for a living." He shook his head.

I nodded, not wanting to start a fight over this. I wanted to leave on a good note, a happy note.

"I do, and I didn't mean anything by it. We both know that being together isn't good for either of us. My therapist told me that—"

He recoiled. "Maybe your therapist is wrong."

The thought had occurred to me.

Would making the right choice hurt this much?

"I'm going back home, Zack. I need family. I need to be surrounded by love."

"And my love isn't good enough?" He cocked his chin slightly.

"We aren't together. It's not the same."

He scratched the dark stubble on his chin and shook his head. "So, you were going to pack up and leave without me knowing?"

"That was the hope." I attempted a feeble smile. "I knew this would hurt too much."

"Then maybe it's the wrong choice." His eyes never wavered from mine.

"You were supposed to be in Alaska this week."

His jaw clenched as he tapped the counter with his knuckle, never taking his gaze away from me.

"I had my brother fly up to finish the job."

"Why?"

"Because I don't want to lose you."

Chapter Two

Zack

It was true. I didn't want to lose her. And now, the thought of Sadie being across the country made me sick to my stomach. She'd been through so much and was the strongest woman I'd ever met.

I loved her more than I knew possible.

I wanted to make this work.

But the reason I came back wasn't to beg her to get back with me. I didn't do that. If what we shared wasn't enough for her, I certainly wouldn't beg for it. I fought for our love, but I'd be damned if I would beg for it.

I returned because I found out the woman who'd kidnapped Sadie was out of jail on a technicality.

"Zack, you know it's over between us," she said softly, her expression falling.

Her throat constricted while she pushed down a hard swallow, which told me she still cared, regardless of her actions.

She didn't want this to be over, either.

But none of that counted.

All that mattered was that Sadie remained safe and unharmed.

Sadie walked over to a small table and sat in a chair, kicking one out in front of her as an invite.

Her striking green eyes took me in as I walked over to take a seat.

"Sadie, I'm going to say this one time." I tilted my head slightly and looked at her. "Your therapist is full of shit, and I love you more than you could understand. Even though I'm afraid I have to disagree, I also respect your decision to end things with me."

She nodded in silence, but I noticed a flicker of

doubt in her eyes.

Sadie cleared her throat and glanced at the clock on the wall, surrounded by two carved grizzly bears and a pine tree motif. This coffee shop usually felt like home, but now it felt like an empty shell of a place I no longer wanted to be, especially if Sadie had no plans to stay.

I cupped my hands and slid them onto the table, wringing them with each passing second. "Sadie, did you hear from the prosecutor this morning?"

I knew the best way to be with Sadie was direct.

Her gaze widened, and she quickly shook her head. "No. Why would I? Did they move up the trial date?"

My heart hammered in my chest as I saw confusion in her eyes.

She didn't know.

"I didn't think I had to go to court until spring at the earliest," she muttered, lifting her gaze.

"It's not that, Sadie. Carmella got out on a technicality."

All the color drained from Sadie's face, and her hands instantly trembled. I shot out of the chair and kneeled before her as she brought her palms over her face.

"No." She shook her head. "No. That's not possible. The prosecutor said he had a solid case."

"He does. He still does, but…" I softly placed my fingers under her chin and tipped her head toward me. I needed her to stay with me, not go back to the place that always pulled her away.

"But what?" Anger flashed through her gaze.

"The police made a mistake that day, and her attorneys caught it." I shook my head. "But the prosecutor is certain he can have Carmella picked up again in a few weeks. It'll be on a lesser charge, but she's still looking at ten years."

"Ten years?" She stiffened. "Ten years? I'll only have peace for ten years?"

I felt the same.

She stood from the chair quickly, and it fell to the floor with a crash as I jumped out of her way.

"I don't understand. Why didn't I get a call?" She dashed to the back of the counter and pulled out her purse, quickly digging through it until she found her phone.

Her expression fell when she looked at the screen. "He must have left a message. I didn't hear it ring. It was during our busy time." Sadie sniffled, and I looked at the floor, wishing I had words to make it all disappear.

"You don't have to do this alone, Sadie." I moved toward her, and she held up her hand.

Sadie's eyes flashed to mine. "I'm more alone than you'll ever understand."

"I can protect you," I said softly, watching her emotions take hold. "I'm here for you."

Her hands shook as she bent over and leaned against the counter, taking a deep breath.

"But I don't think it's a good idea for you to return to New England."

She wiped a stray tear, and I wanted to jump over the counter and bring her into my arms, but she'd made it clear that we were over.

"I'm so tired of being scared, Zack. I'm just... exhausted." Her lip quivered, and it felt like a stab to the gut as a sob fell from her mouth.

Without thinking, I scaled the counter and pulled her into my arms. I felt her body relax as her head rested on my chest. She sniffled, and dampness spread on my shirt as I ran my hands along her dark blonde hair.

My mouth pressed onto the top of her head. The familiar scents of coconut and lime drifted over me. Sadie's favorite body wash. It was even the little things I missed. I took another breath, but I knew to respect her wishes. "Let me help, Sadie. Let me be a part of this. I'll respect whatever boundaries you give me, but I must keep you safe."

She nodded, still pressing her cheek against my chest, and I didn't want to let go. Feeling her in my arms stopped my world, and I knew I'd do everything I could to protect her regardless of whether she agreed.

Sadie sniffled and tilted her head to look at me through her big, green eyes, tears rimming her lids as she let out a shaky breath.

"I need to call my family." She straightened slightly and stepped back, reaching for her phone. "To let them know I won't be coming yet."

I nodded as relief spilled through me, and she

placed her first call.

At least she still trusted in my ability to protect her.

Her sister picked up instantly on the speakerphone, and Sadie started crying.

I pulled her into my arms again as her sister Elena panicked on the other end of the phone.

"Carmella's out." Sadie's words were nearly impossible to understand, but Elena didn't need to hear to know.

"What? That can't be."

"It's true," I replied flatly.

"Zack? You're with her? Thank God." Elena's voice rose. "What happened? What's going on?"

Sadie relayed everything as I let her go, and she mindlessly wandered around the empty coffee shop, weaving through tables and chairs. Occasionally, she'd stop to catch her breath or blow her nose.

"Hey," Melanie said from the back room. "Is everything okay?"

I knew Sadie never said much to her friend about what had happened to her back in New York. Just how does one explain that you'd been kidnapped and almost murdered by a deranged woman?

You didn't.

Melanie's eyes stayed on mine as Sadie kept talking to her sister about the kidnapping.

"Kidnapped?" Melanie's eyes widened with horror as her hands slid to her mouth. "That's why she hated being hugged."

I nodded.

Sadie spun around and froze when she saw Melanie standing near the back room.

"I need to go. Please tell Mom and Dad," Sadie pleaded, but she was too paralyzed that her secret had gotten out.

"Are you...?" Melanie started and then pressed her lips together. "You were...?"

Sadie nodded.

"When you were a child or...?" Melanie's voice softened.

"No. It was about six months ago."

Melanie gasped. Her cheeks reddened. "I'm sorry. I don't even know what to say. I'm just at a loss."

"That's okay." Sadie hugged herself.

She looked like a shell of the woman I saw earlier, her shoulders curled over, her face still pale...

"Where did it happen?" Melanie asked, her gaze bouncing between me and Sadie.

"New York." She licked her lips and tried to push down a swallow. I could tell she was teetering on the edge. "If it hadn't been for Zack and his brother..."

"There was an entire team. I was part of it. Her brother-in-law had his men, the police were involved, and we found her."

Sadie tucked a piece of hair behind her ear and nodded. "But Zack was the one who got me away from the woman."

Melanie couldn't hide her surprise. "It was a woman?"

"And she's out of jail as of yesterday," Sadie whispered, dropping her gaze to the tiled floor.

I couldn't pretend to understand Sadie's fear of knowing she had to look over her shoulder for the next month.

But I had to believe what the prosecutor told me.

He could bring her back in soon.

"Oh, my gosh." Melanie dashed over to Sadie with open arms, but she stopped herself.

A tiny smile surfaced on Sadie's mouth as she hugged Melanie, which I knew was a big step.

Sadie glanced at me as she pulled back from Melanie. "Thanks for coming back to tell me. I don't know what I would have done if I'd returned to my apartment tonight and finally listened to the message."

I scratched my chin and nodded. "Speaking of, I say we go grab what you need from your place and get you settled back at my house."

Sadie narrowed her gaze on me. "At your place?"

"You can stay with me," Melanie offered to Sadie.

My spine stiffened. I couldn't keep an eye on things if she weren't with me. Just the logistics of everything would be a nightmare.

"Although Zack and his brothers do this thing for a living, don't you?" Melanie teased, eyeing me with a coy smile. The town knew Granite Peak Security was the region's top security and protection firm. "If he's offering, I'd take him up on it. But again, my arms are always open."

Sadie slowly brought her gaze to mine, and I saw her body tense slightly. "It probably is for the best."

"Your job is still open here, too," Melanie said softly. "I didn't have the energy to post the job listing."

"I don't think that's—" I stopped speaking when Sadie's eyes narrowed on mine.

"What? Do you think I should just stay locked up at your house until the criminal is locked away again? Never step foot out your front door? Keep the shades drawn?"

And the pistols drawn, I wanted to add. But I knew that wasn't reasonable, even if that was the only way to keep her one hundred percent safe.

Melanie's gaze flicked from Sadie's to mine. "I mean, I don't need an answer right away. Why don't you two get things settled and..."

Sadie folded her arms over her chest and shook her head. "Nope. I need some stability. Some normalcy. And I doubt she'd waste time trying to hunt me down clear across the country."

I stared at Sadie, unsure whether she believed the words coming from her mouth.

Her cheeks reddened, and I knew she didn't.

"We will keep you safe until Carmella's put away. I promise you that," I assured her. "But there will be things put in place for the next few weeks or months that you may not like."

Sadie nodded slowly. "I understand."

"And if there's anything I can do…" Melanie's eyes stayed on mine, and I nodded.

"Fine. Let's get this over with." Sadie let out a sigh. "I sent most of my belongings to my parents' house already, so this shouldn't take long."

My mind flashed back to just six weeks ago when we were still together, and I'd picked her up from her shift here after I'd gotten back from a job in Idaho. Her eyes lit up when she saw me, and I pulled her into my arms, inhaling everything about her as if I'd been away for years. In actuality, it had only been two weeks.

Everything about that night was perfection. I took her to our favorite steak place at the lodge in town. We ate and drank until we could barely move, but we somehow managed to stay up late into the night, making love and promises that she never had any intention of fulfilling.

It was all hard to believe.

Two days later, she dumped me.

And now she was coming back to my house where everything fell apart. I clenched my fists and tried to push away the hurt and longing when I glanced at Sadie.

"You ready?" I asked more gruffly than I intended, but Sadie didn't pick up on it.

She grabbed her purse and gave a flick of her wrist in Melanie's direction. "I'll be here bright and early tomorrow."

Melanie smiled and nodded. "Sounds good, but only if Zack says so. I don't want to do something to jeopardize your safety."

A sly smile slid across Sadie's mouth. "Of course, it's fine with Zack."

She slapped my back and walked in front of me as I drew a deep breath and walked out the door with the love of my life.

Chapter Three

Sadie

Seeing Zack nearly killed me. The hurt in his eyes felt like a million wasps stinging my heart as he followed behind me in his truck to my apartment. My heart pulled when I approached the small building nestled among the trees. I'd had so many good memories here.

It had felt like I was starting over the moment I'd signed my lease, and Zack had been with me every step of the way.

As I pulled into the parking spot in front of my

apartment, Zack pulled in next to me. I caught him glancing at me through the window, and I couldn't help but smile.

Breaking up with him was the hardest thing I ever did, apart from fighting to stay alive. Being kidnapped had been entirely out of my control. But ending things with Zack was completely in my control and decided by me, which made it so difficult.

He walked over and opened the door to my Honda. Our fingers touched as I climbed out of the car, and I instantly felt the pull to him. I shut the door and yanked my hand away.

"This isn't going to be easy, is it?" I grumbled, marching past him toward the front door of my apartment, painted a bright green to match the trim of the building. This apartment complex was a small eight-unit building and looked like a rustic lodge. I'd been looking forward to decorating for my first Christmas here, but that was before everything changed.

It hadn't helped that I'd suddenly heard from someone who had left a bad taste in my past. It was just one more reminder telling me it was time for a change, and I didn't want Zack to get wind of any of it. My life had tipped into the realm of bizarre mortification, and I couldn't just blame bad luck any longer. I had to start taking accountability.

As I put my key in the lock, Zack approached me and shook his head, taking over the job as he pointed for me to stand to the side.

Even though I wanted to protest, I knew he wasn't doing it to be a jerk. This was what he did for a living. This was how he'd saved me in the first place.

By being methodical.

Disciplined.

His hand gripped the doorknob, and he turned it slowly as my heart started to race.

Two minutes ago, it hadn't even occurred to me someone could be waiting inside for me.

Now, reality set in, and dread filled me to the brim. This was going to be my new life until Carmella was arrested again.

And with everything I'd been feeling these last few weeks, my anxiety was just getting started.

I stayed outside as Zack slowly opened the door,

scanning the small apartment, now empty and void of anything that made it mine. His movements were stealthy and calculated as he made his way to the corner wall. He motioned for me to come inside and shut the door as he moved through the rest of the apartment.

Watching him move down the hallway toward my bedroom made my heart sink even lower. This man was risking his life for me yet again.

"Sadie," Zack's voice boomed down the hallway and smacked me with the urgency I feared. "The apartment's clear, but I need you to see something."

My pulse raced as I dashed down the hallway to my bedroom to see Zack standing next to a pile of garbage I certainly hadn't left on the floor.

His eyes met mine as he knelt and picked up some rope. My throat constricted the moment I saw it. The same type that had been wrapped around my wrists and ankles.

Nausea sloshed deep inside me as I tried to focus on what else was in the pile.

Zack shook his head as he tossed the rope aside and rummaged through a lighter, duct tape, plastic, and some empty plastic cups. He reached for a newspaper and held it up, glancing at the front page, and my heart sank.

"None of this is yours," he stated flatly.

A chill ran up my spine as I glanced over my shoulder down the hallway. "Someone was here? What is the paper for?"

He let out a deep sigh and turned it around to reveal the front-page news about my rescue.

"She always threatened that she'd torch the place," I whispered, staring at the lighter. "How did she find me?"

I slumped to my knees next to Zack as the nausea intensified. "Zack, I can't do this. Not again."

He pulled me into him, the warmth of his body shielding me from the chill drifting over me. I felt a tear roll down my cheek, but I pushed it away. I wouldn't give Carmella the gratification of seeing me cry again.

I'd vowed that even when I took the stand as a witness, I wouldn't cry.

"You're going to be okay."

"So, she's here?" I murmured as his arms let me

go.

"I…" He shook his head. "It's hard to believe that she could possibly get here this fast or be this…"

"Stupid?" I asked, my brows arching.

"Yeah."

I clutched myself, crossing my arms over my chest and gripping my shoulders as if that would provide the shield I needed.

Glancing around my nearly empty bedroom that I'd called home for several months made me sad. This was my sacred place—a place where I'd finally found some healing.

And this woman wanted to take that away from me.

Zack stood and walked over to the window, running his finger along the sill. "They didn't use the front door."

I wasn't sure if that made me feel better or worse.

"I don't think this was Carmella." He turned to gauge my reaction, but all I could do was stare straight ahead.

"There's something I haven't mentioned," I said

softly, not meeting Zack's gaze.

Zack walked to the attached bathroom and kneeled at the vanity, opening both doors to reveal nothing.

He turned slowly and nodded. "Now's probably the time to tell me anything and everything."

I laughed softly, seeing his lip curl slightly.

"I was worried I wouldn't hear that again," he said, walking over to me, still kneeling by the pile.

"What?" I asked, shaking my head.

"Your beautiful laughter."

I tilted my head slightly at the gorgeous man before me and wondered why I had given it all up.

It was easy to point the finger at him with my therapist. I could always explain away the night terrors or the flashbacks in the middle of a grocery store because, as my therapist put it, I could never escape the ties to that traumatic event when my rescuer was always there to remind me.

And it wasn't his fault.

The man was built to be a protector.

At over six feet tall, he was lean and muscular,

disciplined, devoted…

But he shouldn't have to play the hero in his personal relationships.

He knelt and brushed away a stray piece of hair from my cheek. "What haven't you told me?"

"Over the last few weeks, I've felt like I'm being watched." My eyes met his, and I caught a flicker of anger whizz through his gaze.

"Let's get your things while you fill me in. I don't want to be here a second longer than we need to be. And we're leaving your car here."

I stomped in protest, and he cocked a brow in my direction as I laughed. "You just bring it out in me. How am I supposed to get to work?"

"I'll drive you," he said gruffly, moving to the closet.

I walked up behind him. "And then what? You sit there all day while I make lattes and serve sandwiches?"

"That's the plan."

"You're being ridiculous," I muttered, reaching for the last few shirts and a couple of pairs of jeans that

I hadn't shipped off to my parents' house.

He opened the pink suitcase I had propped against the wall, and I put my clothes in there before wandering to the bathroom to grab my basket of toiletries.

"Now, tell me, what's been going on?" He towered over me as I put the last few pairs of shoes and two pairs of pajamas in my suitcase.

I sighed before leaving the bedroom to grab the last few photos I kept in the living room, and that should be it. I'd officially have keys to turn in. The pale grey walls no longer looked inviting, and the tiny fireplace in the corner looked suddenly out of place without furniture surrounding it. The cabinets and glass shelves in the kitchen looked empty and sad. It was hard to believe how many hopes, ideas, and wishes for a fresh start were dreamt here.

I spun around to see Zach studying me. He wasn't letting me out of his sight.

"There's not much to tell, Zack. It's probably all in my head. Over the last few weeks, I'd get this strange sensation that someone was watching me. Simple as that."

"Where?"

I shrugged. "Everywhere. It would happen at the store, restaurants, the coffee shop… and every single time, I'd turn around to see absolutely no one."

"And it's been happening for three weeks?" His eyes narrowed on me, and I pushed away the tiny little fact that he always knew when I was stretching the truth to make things seem better than they were.

Because it had been happening for a lot longer.

Even when I was with Zack, I'd started to feel the sensation.

And then I heard from someone who had been silent for years.

I promised myself it was a coincidence, but I didn't even know any longer.

Zack eyed me, and I knew I couldn't lie to him.

Looking around my apartment, I let out a groan of annoyance.

My hands shot into the air and waved around. "No. Fine. It started about a week before I broke up with you."

Horror washed over his face. "And you didn't tell me?"

"Zack, I'm so tired of living in this head of mine, in this swarm of memories, that I didn't even want to vocalize what I was sensing. I already feel crazy enough. It's why..." I stopped myself. I didn't need to go down that path with him.

"It's why what?" he asked, stepping closer.

I tipped my face up to look at him closely and slowly breathed. "It's one of the reasons I knew it was time to leave. To start over. I'm losing my mind, Zack. You don't need to be a part of that."

He straightened and looked around the empty apartment before returning to me.

"How do you explain that pile of shit in your bedroom? That's not in your head. You didn't leave it there." His brows furrowed in frustration, and I suddenly felt guilty for letting him in on my secrets. "For some reason, you're in someone's line of sight, and it's up to me to figure out—"

"No," I interrupted. "It's not up to you. I'm not your responsibility, Zack."

He instantly closed the gap between us as his eyes locked onto mine. I tipped my chin up to see his intense gaze studying me. A wave of longing surfaced.

"You will always be my responsibility, Sadie. I love you. I can't stop loving you." His voice was gruff and direct like it always had been.

"Don't say that," I said, feeling the lump in my throat constrict. "I'm a mess."

"You're not a mess, Sadie. You've never been a mess."

Zack looped his arms around my waist as my lips trembled. "It's in my head, Zack. It has to be. She's been locked up. No one is spying on me."

He slowly licked his bottom lip and looked toward the front door. "I won't even pretend to know what's going on, but if you say you felt someone watching you, I believe it, and we'll solve it. You deserve a normal, healthy, and happy life."

My gaze unexpectedly dipped to his mouth as the familiar pull washed over me. The electricity zipped through my veins as he kept me in his arms.

The only place I felt safe was in Zack's arms. It

had been that way since the kidnapping.

I straightened and brought my eyes to his. "I'm not your responsibility any longer. We broke up."

A smile cracked his steely gaze, and he shook his head. "You broke up with me. It wasn't exactly mutual."

As the feelings for Zack swarmed through with an intensity I didn't expect, I stepped away, and he let go.

"You'll always be mine to protect, even if I'm not yours," Zack said, catching my hand in his. "I mean it. But you made your decision. Once we get through this, you can return to your plans and head back east."

Hearing those words drip from his lips made my heart fall, even though that was precisely my plan. The plan I'd agonized over for the last six weeks.

"Now, let's get out of here and keep you safe," he said, low and in control.

Chapter Four

Zack

"You should have seen the look on her face, Ian. It was like she thought she was in the midst of going crazy and wanted to beat herself up on the way there." I sighed into the speakerphone to my brother. He took over my assignment in Alaska and called to let me know he was returning early.

"She's done that since we've met her, Zack. She still thinks it's her fault that she let someone trick her into being captured." My brother stopped speaking for a second. "And I don't mean that in a bad way. It's just that she always shoulders the weight of the world."

"I know. Now is no different."

"So, you sent the photos of everything to the prosecutor just in case it's connected?"

"I did."

I heard Sadie in the kitchen with the faucet running, singing one of her favorite Christmas songs even though it was only October. "I don't have a good feeling about this."

"Well, it's definitely strange that she's been feeling like someone's watching her. But it couldn't have been Carmella. She's only been out since yesterday."

"No. My instincts tell me it's someone else."

"Agreed."

The water stopped running in the kitchen, and I didn't hear Sadie's singing. "I gotta get some dinner going. I'll see you tomorrow. Maybe stop by here before you head into the office?"

"Will do. Did you want me to stay in the spare house on the property?"

When I first bought this place, it had a smaller home that I'd lived in while I built the home I currently live in. Being that I liked privacy and didn't need any extra income, I'd kept it vacant.

"I don't think so."

"Let me know if things change. I'll see you tomorrow." My brother hung up the phone, and I stood from my desk, glancing at the dark green chenille couch in the corner of my office.

My mind fell back to Sadie in here the first week after she'd moved to Washington. She had on a pair of oversized knit overalls that hung from her curvy body, her hair was in a messy braid, and her big, beautiful eyes seductively watched me work until I couldn't handle it any longer.

I smiled at the thought and shook my head. She'd managed to make me feel like the luckiest man alive in the world. Yet again.

But that was what Sadie did to me.

Always had.

From the moment I saw her photograph when she was missing to seeing her in the warehouse tied up by a vicious woman with a vendetta.

I cleared my throat and walked down the hallway

to the kitchen, where Sadie had a pile of diced peppers in a bowl and a tissue in her hands, dabbing her eyes as a half-cut onion lay on the chopping block.

"Gets you every time," I said, laughing softly as she blinked her teary eyes open to see me.

"If you'd just do my trick of keeping the onions in the fridge, we wouldn't have this problem."

"Man, I missed you," I teased, shaking my head while taking over the task of slicing the onion.

She didn't say anything, and I didn't expect her to. I needed to remember that this wasn't personal.

Her being here was business.

Sadie leaned against the granite counter and smiled. "Things were always easy with you."

I nodded silently and finished slicing the onion. "I have to keep reminding myself that you're here for professional services, nothing more."

She let out a soft sigh and walked over to the coffee pot. "Made you a fresh pot."

Sadie poured herself a cup and added some nonfat milk.

"Thanks." I set the knife down and glanced at

her. "I sent some photos of what we found at your apartment to the prosecutor. Neither of us believes it's Carmella, obviously. But we wouldn't put it past her to have someone on the outside trying to intimidate you."

She laughed nervously and took a sip of coffee. "Well, it's working."

Sadie moved over to the stove and turned on a skillet with oil already in the pan.

"I don't believe that for a second," I said softly, glancing outside to see the dimmed light filtering through the trees as the sun set into the night sky. "Very little ever intimidates you."

Sadie grabbed the vegetables and sliced sausage and dumped them into the oil with a sizzle. She shook some garlic and onion powder over the mixture.

"I think my tough-girl façade is starting to crack, Zack." Her arms crossed her chest, and she let out a deep sigh. "It's one of the many reasons I knew I needed... space."

I nodded. "And now you're stuck with me again."

A wry smile spread across her lips, and I felt that pull that lit every cell in my body like a Christmas tree.

She shrugged and chuckled. "Could be worse."

I took a step closer without thinking. "Yeah?"

Sadie nodded, her eyes connecting to mine as she swallowed back something she wanted to say. I could see it in her eyes.

"You're…" She eyed me suspiciously. "You're what every woman dreams about."

"Not the woman who counts, though."

Her gaze dropped to the floor, and she spun around to stir the food.

Damn it. I needed to cool it.

"My brother's stopping by tomorrow morning."

"Okay, but I need to be at the coffee shop at five."

I smiled, nodding. "Okay, then I'll have him meet me there."

She laughed and shook her head, still facing the cooktop. "You're not going to give up, are you?"

"You mean about keeping an eye on you? No."

"Don't you think this is more than an eye?" She walked over to a cabinet, grabbed a large pot, and filled it with water before setting it on the cooktop to boil.

"It's what I do for every client," I assured her.

"I'm not a client. I certainly don't have the money to pay you for your services."

"It's not about the money when it's someone I care about, Sadie. It wouldn't matter who was in my life and needed some assistance. Your safety is all that matters."

One of the hanging chrysanthemums outside near the double doors swayed in the shadows, and my heart stopped as I glanced around to see still trees and the other hanging baskets frozen in time. A prickle of hesitation ran up my flesh.

No.

The flower basket slowed to a stop, and I moved to the windows, glancing outside. Every inch of my perimeter had cameras and motion sensors, and I didn't receive one alert.

Just because it was Sadie, I still had to stay logical. I couldn't let my emotions get the best of me. It could have been something as simple as a bat running into it.

"Everything okay?" she asked, looking over at me.

I nodded, turning around to see the kitchen drenched in warm hues. From where I stood by the door, Sadie was entirely in my view, looking as stunning as ever.

She'd returned to stirring the pasta, and I couldn't help but notice the gentle sway of her hips as she moved or the humming she did under her breath that she probably didn't even know she was doing.

I smiled and walked over to the cabinets to set the table.

"You really didn't have to make dinner for us." I grabbed some plates and silverware, and she shrugged, still turned away.

"It's the least I could do." She laughed before reaching for a strainer for the pasta. "Here I go and break up with you and then suddenly move in."

Sadie drained the pasta and poured the sausage and veggie mix into the noodles.

"It's nice. I didn't think I'd ever see you back in my house, let alone my kitchen." I caught a glimpse of regret flickering through her gaze. "I mean, I hoped I'd see it, but…"

"But I broke up with you."

"Yeah…" I let out a wistful sigh. "And I didn't think cooking was exactly your favorite thing to do."

Sadie carried over the pot of pasta and sausage and glanced at me as she set down the stainless pot. A wry smile tugged at the corner of her lips, and I spotted the familiar spark that I could never get enough of, even back on that fateful day.

"Well, there's a lot you don't know about me." She pressed her lips together. "I've been doing a lot of soul searching."

Her words stung a little, but I smiled as she took a seat.

I walked to the fridge for some red wine. Sure, we'd only been together for six months, but it was intense and passionate. The moments we spent together were so full of life and talking about dreams and things from our past that it felt like I'd known her forever. It was as if our histories were shared and cemented in something neither of us understood.

And it felt like I knew just about all I could about Sadie.

Except when I didn't. There were plenty of times when she'd clam up. Her expression would change. She'd pull away slightly or change the subject. But she'd always brushed it off to flashbacks, and I certainly wasn't going to press it.

"Indulge me," I said, pouring us each a glass of wine.

"I've had a lot of time to allow myself to… forget." Her eyes met mine, and I felt that familiar sensation that made me want to become a superhero for her and decimate anyone who even looked at her wrong. Even in my line of work, I rarely hated people. But I truly hated Carmella for taking away Sadie's freedom to live without fear. It was bad enough that Sadie would have to relive everything when the trial came up this spring. However, that hung in the balance at this point.

I scooped the pasta onto her plate and then mine as she sipped wine. Her shoulders relaxed.

"This is my favorite wine." She looked at me over the rim of her glass.

I nodded. "I always keep some in the fridge."

Her lips tugged into a beautiful smile. "In case I

stop by?"

"Something like that." I took a bite of pasta and couldn't help but moan in delicious satisfaction. "So, you *can* cook."

Sadie chuckled. "Surprise."

I narrowed my eyes on her and smiled. "You always pretended you weren't that great at it."

"That's because I found out how amazing you are at cooking." Her cheeks flushed, and she laughed. "And I didn't pretend that I wasn't great. I just never offered to do it."

"I've found it helps me decompress. I missed cooking, and I didn't even realize it."

The steely clang of her silverware as she daintily cut one of the sausages echoed just how thick the air was with silenced emotions. We'd never had moments like these where there was so much to say, but neither of us said it.

"So, as I was saying…" She smiled and took another bite. I noticed the little dimple that always surfaced on her right cheek while she chewed.

There wasn't much about Sadie I didn't notice.

But what concerned me were the secrets I felt hiding behind her recent gaze. They weren't there before, and now, with every flick of her eyes, I could tell she had been burying something inside.

"I've been working hard these last few weeks to focus on my future, the move, and trying not to go back to that space, to that time when everything went so wrong."

My chest tightened, watching her relive in those few seconds everything she was speaking about, and I knew she might be right. Her therapist might be onto something. *Maybe I am that constant reminder she doesn't need.*

"And has it been going well?"

She forked a few noodles and peppers. "Sometimes, I can forget and pretend that I was never kidnapped. That my life was as fun-filled and as adventurous as before." Sadie let out a deep breath and took a second before finishing. "And then I wonder if I'm meant to forget it."

I wiped my mouth with the napkin and nodded. "I don't know if you can forget something like that,

Sadie. I'm no licensed therapist, but I don't know if that's a realistic goal. You went through something that shifted how you saw the world."

"Agreed," she said, glancing out the window.

Sadie stiffened, and I followed her gaze.

"Everything okay?"

The hanging baskets were still motionless.

"No. Yes." She rolled her eyes. "Just my mind playing tricks on me again."

"Tell me what you think you saw?"

Sadie reached for the bottle of wine and poured more into her glass. "I thought I saw like a flicker of light or something." She set the bottle down. "But being that you're in the middle of nowhere with a security system that chimes, sings, and throws grenades, I know it's in my head."

I chuckled at the last accusation. "I don't think it's legal to have grenades or bombs on the property."

"But if you could, you would." She laughed nervously, but I saw her gaze linger outside.

"For the record, I only have this much equipment because my brother and I test everything out before we use it for clients."

"Whatever you say, Zack," she teased, and it suddenly felt like old times.

She gasped, and I followed her gaze to see the same flickering light she mentioned.

We were sitting ducks. Every move in this house was lit up like a spotlight, and I saw nothing but shadows of Douglas firs and pines.

I stood slowly and went to the wall to flip the switch for the exterior lights, and the entire backyard lit up like a carnival.

"What is that?" Sadie asked with the ghost of vulnerability surfacing.

Chapter Five

Sadie

The entire woods behind his home sprang to life like it was daylight.

Staring back at us was a giant black bear who started backing up.

"It's been tagged. We were catching the light from the metal on its ear."

It felt like the most significant weight had been lifted from my shoulders as he flipped the lights off to leave the bear alone.

"When did you install the exteriors to the forest?"

Zack scratched his chin and took a seat back at the table. "A few weeks back. I wanted patio lighting, and then I was like, why stop there?"

I chuckled and shook my head. "Sounds about right. I can't even begin to tell you how amazing I feel knowing it's just a black bear. Like, that is what my life has come to. I'm relieved a bear is staring at me for dinner."

Zack laughed. "Yeah. That says a lot."

The look in his eyes told me he was as worried as I was, which was precisely what I'd wanted to avoid. I was so tired of my problems becoming his problems.

It was one of the reasons I started taking Jiu-Jitsu. I didn't want to feel like I needed to be protected. I wanted to take care of problems myself.

Yet, here I was at my ex's house, and he protected me.

"Does it just come naturally?" I asked.

"What?" he asked, taking another bite of dinner.

"Playing the hero."

He put his fork down and shook his head. "I've never wanted to be a hero. I just want to help people."

I nodded, debating whether to share what I'd been thinking about these last several weeks. I'd been through so much, and my story had a happy ending. More and more, I felt like I should do something about that and help others rather than sink into my fear.

"I do, too, actually." I took a deep breath. "Putting stalker bears aside, I feel like there has to be some purpose to what I went through, even if I'm the one who needs to find it."

Zack nodded slowly. "I get that. What have you been thinking about?"

This was why I loved Zack so profoundly. The conversation just flowed. He had a genuine interest in me. But we had all this baggage and suffering between us, and I knew that I needed separation between my partner and my trauma.

I looked away as I fidgeted. I hadn't voiced these new dreams aloud. "I would love to find a way to create a place where people can go to heal, like maybe a farm or an animal sanctuary." I laughed and brought my gaze to his. "But first, I need to go back to college. I want to become a therapist."

"You never cease to amaze me, Sadie." He tapped his finger on the table and smiled.

"I haven't done it yet, Zack."

His smile grew. "No, but you dared to dream it."

I straightened in my chair and suddenly felt as crazy as my thoughts were, that maybe there was a piece of my idea that could come true. "First, I just need to get Carmella back where she belongs."

"Agreed." His jaw tensed, and I noticed the same look of disgust that would wash over his face whenever Carmella was brought up.

"Anyway, that's my hope… that someday, I can buy a huge piece of property in New Hampshire or somewhere and welcome people to heal."

Zack nodded, dropping his gaze. "You know, I have forty acres here." He brought his hazel eyes to mine, and that familiar stir of warmth pooled in my belly.

I nodded with a laugh. "Right. You do, Zack. And that's awesome for you."

He chuckled. "Just throwing it out there."

I cleared my throat and stood up, feeling a flush of longing wash through me as his gaze fell along my body.

"This isn't going to be easy, is it?" I asked, reaching for my empty plate to take to the sink.

"Which part?" He ran his palm along his chiseled jaw, and images of him scattering kisses along my naked body forced their way into my mind. He caught my expression and cocked his head slightly. "What? Something has you blushing."

"Nothing at all." I chuckled, spinning on my heels and taking my dirty dish to the sink.

He came up behind me, and I felt the heat of his body as he stretched his arms around me to put his plate into the sink. Facing the kitchen sink, I closed my eyes and inhaled everything about him since he couldn't see my face.

The faint smell of soap and a woodsy smell surrounded me as his closeness made my body respond in ways it hadn't since we broke up.

I blinked my eyes open and spun around to have him only inches from my face.

He smirked, realizing the effect he had on me. "You're in my way."

My brows shot up. "How so?"

"You cooked. I'll do the dishes." His coy smile grew. "Just like old times."

"Old times." I nodded, pressing my lips together.

His fingers grazed my arms, and a hiss of electricity shot through me from his touch. I knew I needed to leave him to the dishes, or tonight might end precisely how it would when we were together.

Clothes hurriedly thrown everywhere.

Pillows on the floor.

Blankets barely clinging to the bed.

I bit my lip to hide my smile at the memories and lowered my brows. "Excuse me. I think it's time I go into the family room and stare mindlessly at the television."

He raised his arms, unboxing me from the sink, and nodded. "Your wish is my command, Sadie. Always will be."

I wanted nothing more than to fall into his arms and kiss him, but it wouldn't be fair to him. I'd broken things off with him, and I wasn't in the habit of playing games.

As I walked out of the kitchen, a little thrill ran

through me as I realized he was watching me leave, and I couldn't help but sway my hips a little more at the thought.

But the moment I'd collapsed on the familiar couch and tugged on my favorite throw before grabbing the remote, my mind spiraled back to where it had wanted to be for months.

Reliving the fear, the emotional pain, the physical hurt.

The nightmares.

The anxiety.

And now my captor was walking the streets somewhere, and my apartment here in a remote mountain town had already been targeted.

It didn't help that Carmella had been heavily connected to New York politics. She had a lot of dirt on many influential and wealthy people. Maybe one of them worried I knew more than I did.

The thought sent a chill through me.

I pulled the blanket up higher and hugged myself as I forced my mind blank.

This constant rehashing exhausted me. I only

wanted to stare at the television and watch something to take my mind off my capture.

It had all been meticulously planned, and it wasn't even about me.

My sister had been working on a story about our late cousin. She'd dug too deep into the mayor's background, along with one of the prominent Mafias left in New York.

However, we soon learned that the Volkov brothers, who ran the notorious crime ring, weren't the culprits. They were crucial figures who'd helped to save my life.

I'd learned that appearances were often deceiving.

And now my sister was married to one of the Volkov brothers.

I'd been staring at the wall for so long that I hadn't even realized that Zack was standing beside me with a bowl of my favorite ice cream until he cleared his throat.

"I thought this might make you feel better."

I reached out for the bowl and smiled. "Thanks."

"If this is too hard being here with me, my brother would be more than happy to have you at his place. While doing the dishes, I realized how selfish I was for bringing you to my house. But I have tunnel vision, and all I want to do is keep you safe."

I took a bite of strawberry ice cream and closed my eyes. "This hits the spot, and I doubt he'd spoil me like you do."

I blinked open my eyes to see him smiling at me. "True."

"No. I'm a big girl." I shrugged. "And hopefully, I won't be here long. I don't want to be an imposition on you any more than I already have."

That same sentiment went for all the people I cared about. When my sister told me she was flying out here immediately, I made her promise she wouldn't.

Zack knelt next to me, and our faces were merely inches apart. The sudden pull between us became undeniable as my body heated, and his hand instinctively moved to my knee.

I wanted to lean into his touch, but I knew better. I understood where it would get us.

"Sadie, you're never an imposition. You will always be a priority to me."

I shook my head slowly. "Not always, Zack. I promise you that. I can take care of myself. Even now."

He nodded and drew a breath. "I fully believe that, but I also don't believe in tempting fate."

For the last several weeks, I'd been on edge and worried that someone was always lurking in the corners, and tonight was the first night that I felt like I could finally breathe again.

And I'd be lying to myself if I didn't admit it was because Zack always felt like home for me.

He comforted me.

He protected me.

He took care of me.

But I knew there was nothing I could do to make things up to him.

"And someday, I hope to repay you." I took another bite of ice cream. "I just don't know how yet."

"Just being you is more than enough, Sadie." His hand slid a little on my knee, and desire shot through me.

My cell buzzed in my back pocket, and Zack

removed his hand so I could answer it.

I didn't recognize the number, but I answered anyway, considering everything happening.

I mindlessly answered on speakerphone when a woman's voice drawled my name.

The air in the room chilled as my eyes darted to Zack's. He started recording our call on his phone, and I nodded.

"Who is this?" I asked, recognizing Carmella's voice immediately.

"Your friend and longtime companion." She laughed the familiar cackle that slammed me back to the warehouse she'd kept me in.

My body trembled as I stared at my phone, willing her to disappear.

"What do you want?" I tried to keep my voice steady. I would never let this woman know the fear and pain she'd caused me.

"Just a friendly call to let you know that I've forgiven you."

"Forgiven me?" I choked out.

"Yes. I've forgiven, but I will never forget." She

stayed silent for a few seconds. "I've heard Washington is a lovely place to visit this time of year."

"I wouldn't know."

"Of course you would. But we won't go into that. I have dinner to go to in the city. I just wanted to touch base with you since I'm out now, and I have no intentions of going back. Good night."

I didn't say a word and waited for her to hang up as my pulse pounded heavily and the nightmare of my life swirled around me.

Handing my half-eaten ice cream to Zack, I stood and wandered to the window overlooking the back yard. It was as if I half expected her to come running up to the glass to scare me.

Zack stood behind me and drew in a deep breath. "She's brazen."

I shrugged and nodded. "Always has been. Do you think she's here?"

"I don't know. It's seven here and ten o'clock back in New York. Kind of late for dinner."

"New Yorkers eat late all the time."

He rested his hand on my shoulder. "Yeah. But

it's not too late to let the prosecutor know."

I shook my head, trying to massage the ache away from my temples. "This just doesn't make sense."

"It doesn't. She's smarter than this." He removed his hand from my shoulder. "But we need to stay vigilant. I'll send the prosecutor the recording so that he has it and understands what we're dealing with."

I turned to look at Zack. "Thank you. Thank you for everything."

"You never have to thank me, Sadie. You mean so much to me. You always will."

Chapter Six

Zack

I couldn't fall asleep as my mind rehashed everything from tonight. As I lay in bed, the house's silence was almost deafening. I'd quietly checked on Sadie more times than I could count, which was ridiculous since her guestroom was secured entirely along with the entire home. Between the state-of-the-art security system and automatically locking interior doors, there was little I had to worry about.

When my mind had almost let me rest, an eerie

sensation shot me out of bed. I glanced around the darkened room as my heart rate jumped and my consciousness became less foggy.

Whatever bothered me wasn't from inside this house, and it wasn't a friendly black bear this time. I knew it deep in my soul. Ever since I was young, my brother and I had been taught to home in on our instincts. Our parents never told us why we needed to trust our gut until we were much older, close to adulthood. The reason shocked us, but it made us both grateful for our fine-tuned instincts.

And now was no different.

In the shadows, I moved to the window and glanced outside.

Nothing caught my eye.

I made my way out of my bedroom and down the hall toward Sadie's. I didn't want to worry her, but I did want to ensure her safety. I quietly opened her door and locked it from the inside with a code. She could get out, but there was no way anyone was getting in once this door was shut.

The unsettling feeling only got stronger as I made

my way down the stairs to the kitchen. Only a soft, ambient glow came from the undercabinet lighting left on earlier. The blinds and curtains had all been shut. I went to my office and opened a cabinet to reveal the property's cameras. Everything looked fine.

But I knew it wasn't.

I grabbed my Glock 19 out of the safe and made my way toward the garage, where I exited through a side door before rearming the security system.

The moon cast an ashen, eerie light over the ground as I snaked out of sight. It no longer felt like the only thing I'd meet tonight was a black bear.

With each step toward the woods, the forest felt less welcoming. I hesitated and glanced back at the house.

Sadie would be okay.

Yet apprehension clawed at me, becoming more pronounced with each second. Even with years of training, I knew someone who didn't belong on this property was out here.

But why?

It could be some random teenagers looking to

make a night out of it, but that rarely happened in this town. All the kids were pretty good.

Each step was done with deliberate care as I made sure to walk on grass until I could get to the quiet mud of the woods, careful to miss any rogue pinecones as I directed myself into the shadows of my surroundings.

Echoing silence surrounded me as I worked through the maze of darkness until an abrupt snap cracked the stillness in front of me.

Someone or something had stepped on a twig, fracturing the silence surrounding me. My gaze darted all around me as my pulse quickened. It was still pretty far ahead.

I stayed frozen for a few minutes as my ears strained to capture any whisper of movement.

And then the shuffling of gravel carried toward me through the night air, and I knew I wasn't alone out here.

My pulse steadied now that I had a location and a plan. The only graveled area was near the tiny house. No animal would make that much noise and give away their location.

I slowly snuck toward the vacant house, darting between trees, moving with a predatory covertness.

Years of training and endless missions with complicated clients had gifted me with the skills of patience and persistence. Slow and steady in my line of work always won the race.

The sound of another twig snapping gave way as I ensured each of my steps didn't become an alarm bell to the intruder, whoever they were.

I'd delved deeper into the woods, careful not to rustle any autumn leaves still clinging to the surrounding maples, when I spotted the small house in the distance. I scanned the long gravel drive and realized how ghostly the vacant house suddenly looked.

Standing against a massive Douglas fir, I pressed myself along the wide trunk as I glanced toward the driveway.

A willowy figure stood on the front porch, faintly illuminated by the moon's glow from the clearing in the woods surrounding the house. I narrowed my eyes as their posture suggested an assuredness that made no sense. I slowly approached the building, crouching as I ducked to stay out of view.

The closer I got, the more assured I was that I was looking at a woman. The figure's curves didn't match any male I knew, and the persistent tapping of her foot seemed to convey some annoyance as if they were waiting for someone inside to answer the door.

So, she wasn't alone.

I edged closer before slinking along the side of the house. I only had one shot at this, and if Carmella made the wrong move, she wouldn't have to worry about her next trial date.

But I also needed to worry about whoever was inside the house.

My mind raced with certainty and conviction that whoever was here was here for Sadie. This person was no casual trespasser, no teenagers looking for a good time.

As I turned the corner of the house and snaked along the front, I saw a beam of light in the person's hand and recognized their cell phone lighting up. I froze so my movement wouldn't give me away with the new reckoning of shadows.

The woman sighed and muttered something under her breath, and I suddenly realized it wasn't Carmella.

She turned to look back down the drive, where I spotted a car tucked under a tree. Her posture stiffened, and dread ran through me as she scanned the property.

Had this intruder sensed me?

I pulled myself closer to the underbrush of the rhododendrons that flanked the landscape as the woman spun around and started toward the vehicle.

I certainly wasn't going to let her get away.

When I realized her guard was down, I rushed toward the woman and quickly apprehended her without even a struggle. Keeping her wrists clutched with my hands, she quickly knelt on the gravel and hissed in pain.

"Ouch. Let go of me. Leave me alone."

I instantly recoiled but quickly pulled up the woman by her wrists as shock washed over me.

"Elena, what the hell are you doing here?" I let go of her and took a step back, smiling.

"Do you always go creeping around your house

at night?" she asked with raised brows.

"This isn't my house." I shook my head.

She scowled. "Then what are you doing here?"

"Well, it's my house, but it's not the one I live in." I glanced at the small building and shook my head.

She nodded and smiled. "It was the only address I could find. I booked a flight out here when Sadie told me Carmella was released, but she told me not to come."

"Sounds about right."

Elena shrugged. "So, I figured if I just showed up, she wouldn't turn me away. I didn't expect you to have multiple houses. Although, this place looked much smaller than what Sadie told me about."

"I'm just so glad it's you, Elena."

"Who else would it be?" She glanced at her car. "I mean, you don't think Carmella will come after Sadie again, do you? What would be the point? She's going back to jail. She'd be foolish to even glance in Sadie's direction."

I nodded silently, knowing if she genuinely believed that, she wouldn't have shown up in the middle of the night to see her sister.

"We got a call tonight from Carmella, but it's freezing outside. Let's get you inside my real house, and I can fill you in."

Even in the night's shadows, I could see all the color drained from Elena's face.

"Wanna just walk back through the woods with me and leave your rental car here, or do you want to drive?"

"Let's drive so I don't have to haul my luggage through the forest. I don't feel like getting muddy at two in the morning."

"How did you know I was here?" she asked as we climbed into her rental car.

I eyed Sadie's sister and shook my head. "I got a feeling someone was on my property before you even appeared on the cameras."

"So, a Spidey sense?" Her right brow curved as she reversed down the long gravel driveway.

"Something like that." I shook my head. "But your sister is sleeping soundly, and the alarm is on."

Elena sighed as I pointed down a different drive flanked by a security gate. "I'm sorry things didn't work out with my sister. I was taken by surprise when I got the call."

I laughed and shook my head. "Not the direction I thought our conversation would go right now."

She grinned. "I'm a hopeless romantic. What can I say? Ever since she told me the news, I've been hugely bummed. You two are meant to be."

I nodded, pressing my lips together. "Thanks for that. I tend to agree."

She slowed at the keypad and glanced at me, and I relayed the guest code to her.

"I bet she'll be so happy to see you."

"Or she'll be extremely annoyed."

"Yeah." I laughed, nodding and looking to see the silhouette of my house materializing in the distance. "It could go either way."

"Let's not wake her until morning."

I watched the gate behind us shut from the side mirror as Elena entered the drive.

Usually, my house felt like a sanctuary, a haven after a long day's work, but tonight, it felt even more like a refuge.

"Do you always find yourself sneaking around your property at night?"

I shook my head as she pulled in front of my garage. "Rarely."

"You still love my sister, don't you?" she asked, turning off the car.

I unbuckled and turned in the seat. "More than anything in this world, and I will do everything within my power to protect her and provide the peace that is her right."

"You're such a good guy, Zack." She nodded. "And Sadie knows that too. She's just…"

"You don't have to explain. She experienced something no one should ever have to go through."

Elena nodded and sighed as we got out of the car. I walked to the trunk as it lifted and took out two large suitcases.

She chuckled and shrugged. "I wasn't sure how long I might be staying."

"I have plenty of room for as long as you need."

"My husband is coming tomorrow. There was only one seat available on tonight's flight."

I always liked Jaxson. He was on the opposite side of where I stood on many things, but his moral compass was pointed in the right direction.

And I knew he'd do anything in his family's power to make this right for Sadie.

"There's room at the resort tomorrow, but tonight, they were booked," Elena explained.

"Nonsense. Stay here. The less you're scattered, the better." I walked up to the front door, pressed the code into the electronic lock, and quickly went inside to turn off the security system as Elena shut the door behind me.

"Beautiful home, Zack."

"Thanks." I grinned. "My brother and I spent so much of our childhood moving around that I knew once I was an adult, I'd find myself a place and plant there."

She nodded, taking in the foyer. "It's a lovely place to plant."

"Do you need anything to drink or snack on or…?"

"I don't, but thanks for offering."

"Absolutely. I'll show you to one of the guest

rooms. It's near Sadie."

"Perfect, and maybe you can fill me in on what happened earlier this evening," she said softly as we climbed the stairs.

"Absolutely." I nodded. "It's probably good that your husband will be here too."

"That's what I was afraid of," she muttered.

And we both knew the nightmare was starting all over again.

Only this time, we didn't know why.

Chapter Seven

Sadie

The sunlight barely filtered in through the sheer curtains. It was too early yet to be woken by the light outside, but I promised Melanie I'd be at the shop at my regular shift. Boy, how quickly things had changed in the last twenty-four hours.

I certainly never thought I'd wake up at my exboyfriend's home.

I'd never spent a night at Zack's in one of his

guest rooms. Usually, I'd wake up cuddled in his arms, taking in the beautiful view of the forest outside his window. But I'd made the decision that led to the guest room, and with everything going on, it was the right decision, even after consuming too much wine last night.

No matter how much I tried to make sense of what was happening in my life all over again, I couldn't. There was no intelligent or logical reason that Carmella would reach out to me. She'd only hurt herself.

Yet, she did.

But I also awoke with such an unusual sensation of sleeping amazingly well, which made no sense. A weightlessness danced around me as I stretched toward the ceiling. I pushed the cold sheets from my skin and took a deep breath. The calmness and peace were a gift this morning, but I knew they wouldn't last.

I stood slowly and savored the blissful moment surrounding me. Maybe it was merely being in Zack's house again. But as each minute ticked by, the memory from last night awoke the familiar creeping sensation that managed to haunt my every thought as reality set in.

I was in hiding, an actual person in hiding. I

wasn't drawn into some maze of a metaphorical demon of the past. No, I was physically hiding from someone who never offered thinly veiled threats.

So, Zack had to be why I had such a blissful sleep. Or maybe my body and soul had finally reached an exhaustion that no longer allowed me to feel.

Maybe this wasn't bliss, but numbness.

My feet hit the cold wooden floor as I went to the bathroom. The cool morning air was still thick in the room. I turned on the hot water in the shower and brushed my teeth while trying to get Zack out of my head.

Usually, our mornings would be filled with something physical that always left me wanting more of him while I was at the coffee shop or while he was heading to some client in another state. But that was just it. So often, I was alone. I'd only get to remember his touch from the morning, and that would have to be enough for weeks.

When we first started dating, I didn't think that would be a problem. I liked my independence and having time to myself.

Or at least I had.

But as each month ticked by, I realized that my life and my needs had severely changed since my incident. And suddenly, being left alone to stir in my own thoughts quietly didn't always lead to great things. The first few months, I wanted to believe it would change, and the last few months, I realized it might be my new normal.

And I needed a partner who was closer.

As I stepped into the steaming shower, I let the water drip down my body as I reminded myself to quit focusing on the past and what led to the breakup. There were a million reasons that got me to where I was now, and I couldn't keep second-guessing.

I quickly rinsed my hair and dried off before sitting at the vanity with a towel wrapped around my body and wet hair dangling along my shoulders. Running a quick brush through it, I spun it into a bun, dabbed some lipstick on, and mentally promised myself that today would be a good day.

I glanced at my phone and saw a message from the prosecutor, and my heart dropped. So much for the good day omen.

I pulled on a cream sweater and jeans when voices drifted up from below. I couldn't hear anything, but I knew there was a woman's voice, and my heart dropped.

I took a deep breath, reminding myself that Zack was single. I had made him that way.

But I couldn't help myself and opened the door, slowly making my way down the hall to hear the voices more clearly.

I noted a sense of urgency, which only made me more curious.

My mind raced with different scenarios. Was it someone he could have dated before? Should I stay upstairs? Or should I be extra loud as I come down the stairs?

No. I was a big girl. *Anyone who's down there must be a friend of his, so she's a friend of mine.*

With that last thought, I made my way down the hall and skipped down the stairs as the voices became clearer.

Elena.

Relief flooded through me until I heard her speak.

"She's going to need our support, no doubt. But she shouldn't be working. She needs to stay here until everything is figured out."

Zack laughed. "You try to tell her that. I was outvoted in that conversation."

"It doesn't matter. She's not going."

I entered the kitchen to see my sister's arms crossed over her chest, a scowl plastered on her face, and a resigned Zack staring back at her.

When his gaze caught mine, a rush of butterflies battled it out in my stomach. The stormy look in his gaze made my entire body respond. After this many months, I would have thought lust would have dropped out of the equation.

But it didn't help that his towering presence and muscular forearms peeked from his grey plaid flannel.

A smile touched his lips as Elena turned to see me.

Her scowl immediately turned into my sister's famous grin as her arms flew in the air and she rushed over to hug me.

"Surprise." She hugged me tight, and I tried not to stiffen as the warmth of her embrace comforted me.

"I told you not to come."

She took a step back and laughed. "And when do I ever listen?"

"So, it's a family trait?" Zack teased, his eyes staying on mine.

"For the record, I'm going to the coffee shop. I'm not going to sit here and twiddle my thumbs all day long."

"I don't like it." Elena shook her head. "And I'm your big sister."

I reached for a banana from the kitchen island. "Tough bananas."

Zack chuckled as I took a bite.

"Besides, Zack is going to be there."

Elena looked over at him, and he nodded. "All day. In fact, my brother's going to meet me there this morning."

"As long as you're buying lattes and croissants, you're more than welcome there too." I smiled at my sister.

"I just might take you up on that since I flew all the way across the country not to let you out of my sight."

"Speaking of, I saw a message from the attorney. I haven't listened to it yet. I didn't want to ruin my good morning."

Zack gave me a sympathetic smile. "It's actually good news. Carmella is not here. They have eyes on her in Brooklyn."

It was like the weight of the world lifted for the day, and I could take a deep breath again.

"Seriously? It's like I hit the lottery."

Elena rubbed her hand along my arm and shook her head. "Soon, you won't have to worry about any of this. I'm sure of it."

I nodded quietly and glanced at the clock on the wall. "I'm actually glad to have you here, but I don't want to be late. Melanie's counting on me."

Elena smiled and took a step back as I finished my banana. "Jaxson will be here in a couple of hours, and then maybe we'll head out to get some coffee?"

"Just let me know when you leave, and I can arm

the house remotely," Zack said, grabbing his jacket.

"Will do." Elena gave me another quick hug, and I followed Zack down the hallway to the garage.

"When did she get here?" I asked the moment we were inside his car.

The large garage door opened, and he pulled out into his driveway.

"Late last night when you were sleeping."

"And you knew?" I asked, eyeing him.

It was unlike Zack to keep secrets from me.

"Didn't have a clue." He laughed, scratching his chin. "In fact, she went to the old house on the property."

"Did she call you?" I asked, glancing out the window as he drove down the winding mountain road flanked with boulders and majestic Douglas firs, cedars, and maples. It was such a beautiful place to live, and I'd miss it on many levels.

"No. I had this feeling that someone was on the property, but the cameras hadn't picked anyone up, so I went out to look."

My eyes widened. "While I was sleeping?"

"Yeah. I had the security system on. You were

safe."

I chuckled. "That wasn't what I was worried about. I don't like the idea of you out there alone." I shrugged, looking at the tiny wrinkles around his eyes as he smiled.

The sun moved higher in the sky, finally casting a golden glow through the towering fir trees as we came to the town of Granite Peak.

"Tell me," I said, eyeing Zack. "What's the plan for the day?"

I pulled my sunglasses on as he smiled.

"Stare at you all day," he joked.

I rolled my eyes, but I couldn't hide my smile.

"Kidding. In all seriousness, since we're stuck together, I thought I would stay in the corner and keep to myself, keep out of your hair, and just get some work done I've been putting off these last few months."

"Sounds good." I nodded.

"Maybe I can convince you to let me take you to lunch." The familiar twinkle in Zack's eyes surfaced, and I slipped my sunglasses off.

"Are you mixing business with pleasure?"

He smiled wider but didn't say a word.

My brows raised as my heart quickened at the memory of how things used to be. It wasn't unheard of for Zack to swing by the coffee shop and take me out for lunch before he had to catch a flight.

"It's hard not to sink into memories, isn't it?" he asked softly, glancing at me.

"Hazard of the job, I suppose."

With his hands on the wheel, he leaned over, his lips close to my ear. The heat and tingle of his breath electrified me as much as his words.

"Remember when I picked you up for lunch, and we got caught in that insane rainstorm?"

My cheeks instantly flushed. "And you missed your flight out of town?"

He straightened and nodded. "But not because of the rainstorm."

I laughed, feeling the wave of nostalgia coat every part of me.

We'd somehow made it back to his SUV, completely drenched, and what started with trying to dry off quickly turned into something I'll never forget.

A thrill ran through me as I recalled the excitement of it all as we somehow managed to get in the back seats while I prayed the tinted windows shielded everything. Our saving grace was probably the storm outside that kept everyone off the sidewalks.

"That was intense." He flashed a roguish grin at me, and another thrill shot through me.

"The weather report calls for a chance of rain today. You know. Just sayin'."

I laughed and shook my head as the coffee shop came into view. "Too bad we aren't in your big SUV."

He smiled, gripping the wheel as he parked along the side street.

"Are you sure you want to stay here all day? We know Carmella isn't here."

The smile quickly left Zack's features, and he nodded. "But we don't know who left those items in your apartment."

I sighed and nodded, knowing he was right. As I unbuckled, I looked back at Zack. "Remember that night we slept under the stars on your patio?"

He nodded, his eyes locked onto mine. "I

wouldn't exactly call it sleeping."

Zack trailed his fingers down over my sweater. "I'm not sure which of us is having it worse, Sadie."

I scowled. "What's that supposed to mean?"

"I don't think either of us is ready to move on."

Tension roiled through me because he was right. "It's not about being ready to move on, Zack. It was never about that."

He nodded, his eyes lingering on mine as he turned off the vehicle.

But I couldn't do this. Not right here.

I hopped out of the SUV, and he hurried to keep up with me.

"I won't apologize for loving you, but I'm sorry for not maintaining professionalism."

I turned and faced him on the sidewalk. "Zack, I love you now more than I ever have, but I don't know that love is enough to heal the mess of a human I've become."

He let out a deep sigh, but he didn't say a word and followed me to the entrance of the coffee shop. Neither of us expected to find the horrors waiting ahead.

Chapter Eight

Zack

"This has nothing to do with Melanie and everything to do with Sadie." I stared at my brother, who'd just happened to get to the coffee shop early to take in the devastation.

He scratched the stubble on his chin and stared at the shattered glass on the wood floors while Melanie and Sadie comforted each other in the corner of the shop near the espresso machines.

Two police officers were inside, looking for clues.

"You can't be sure of that," Ian said quietly. "It could have just been a couple of teenagers or just a completely random druggie to get at some cash."

I glanced inside to see the tables turned on their sides and the chairs upside down, but apart from the broken glass, there wasn't anything else askew.

Except for the safe.

Melanie had relayed that someone managed to crack the safe and take about a grand that she'd had in there from the previous day's closing.

"Listen, you're on high alert because of Sadie, and I get that. But we can't let things distort reality. It's very unlikely that this was directed at Sadie."

I nodded, unconvinced. "But how often do you hear of someone actually able to crack open a safe? Especially nowadays? They'll pry it from the deadbolts in the ground before they actually crack it."

"Our job is to stay impartial. Look at the facts. Protect our client." He caught my gaze, but I didn't say anything. "Your client is Sadie, and if you start mistakenly chasing every lead, you'll miss the most important ones right in front of you."

I heard the words my brother spoke, but I didn't believe them. I knew in my heart that this had everything to do with Sadie.

"My gut tells me otherwise," I said flatly.

"Maybe so, or it could be fear."

I shook my head. "Our parents taught us how to tell the difference."

"But it has never involved someone we love."

I looked up at the overcast sky as the chill in the air picked up.

The two officers stepped outside and glanced at Ian and then at me.

"I don't think this was random," Officer Carl announced. He was the oldest on Granite Peak's police force and had been serving since I was a teenager. Carl was calculating and rarely missed an opportunity to solve a case, even if the crime was a stolen pack of gum.

I lifted my brows and glanced at my brother.

"Why would someone target Melanie?" my brother asked, rocking back on his boots.

"I don't believe she was the target," the officer said flatly.

A knot squeezed tighter in my stomach. "Then who was?"

Officer Carl glanced at Tom, the younger officer. "I think it was your girlfriend."

I shook my head. "We're not together."

Carl stared at me. "She said she was at your house last night?"

"It's complicated."

Officer Carl chuckled. "Isn't it always?"

I folded my arms. "Tell me what you know."

"I'd rather show you. Meet us at the department in an hour. I'll have everything set up. Maybe you'll be able to help us identify who we saw." He glanced at Melanie. "And just bring Sadie. I think Melanie is a little too shaken."

I nodded, looking over at Sadie, who was now stationed behind the espresso machine.

A small crowd of people congregated behind us. Carl scanned the people, mostly locals.

"Nothing much to see here, folks. We've got it handled, and Granite Beans Coffee Shop will be open soon."

Things like this rarely happened in this remote mountain town, so I could feel everyone's tension.

I walked into the coffee shop, crunching on the glass as Melanie slowly walked over with a broom and dustpan.

"I got that," I said, taking them from her. "Why don't you have a seat and decompress?"

A grateful expression traced her features as Sadie walked over and patted her back. "Why don't you take the day off? I can handle things. The repairmen for the glass said they'd be here in a few hours. I can cover."

Melanie shook her head and let out a groan. "No. Then I'd just be at home, stewing over everything."

Sadie nodded sympathetically. "Our mind can be our own worst enemy at times."

Melanie let out a sigh and walked back behind the counter, where she filled up a plastic cup with ice and water and took a drink.

"You doing okay?" I asked Sadie.

It was the first time we had been alone since we saw the coffee shop in shambles.

She squeezed herself and turned at her waist,

looking up at me. "Not really."

"I feel like I brought this on her. She didn't deserve this."

"We don't know that you were the target. Maybe it was a random burglary," I told her, realizing I sounded just like my brother trying to placate me.

Her brow arched slightly, and her glorious eyes lit up. "You don't believe that for a second."

I shook my head with a low growl of a chuckle. "No, I don't."

Sadie picked up the broom that Melanie had left propped on the table and began sweeping all the shattered glass.

"Here, let me do that." I pulled the broom away and took over as she walked over to Melanie, giving her another hug.

My brother watched me from the entrance and smiled. "Melanie's holding up pretty well."

I glanced at Melanie holding her head while Sadie comforted her.

"If you say so."

A van pulled up out front with a glass and mirror

logo, and the passenger got out of the van.

He saw me through the open door and waved. "Hey, we'll take care of all that. We have an industrial vacuum."

I nodded, taking the broom to the back room, and glanced around the storage space. Nothing looked disturbed or out of the ordinary on a shelf where some bags of beans had been tipped over. I spotted the small open safe behind the metal shelving rack, which struck me oddly. Whoever came in search of that safe would have needed to know where it was located.

I set the broom and dustpan against the wall and looked around the space.

Something didn't feel right.

There was a small mirror behind me on the wall, a sketch of a coffee bean next to it, and a few scuffs on the paint from being in a storage room.

"Hey, Zack." Ian walked in and glanced around. "This room fared a lot better than out there."

I nodded and pointed to the safe. "Odd that someone knew where the safe was."

Ian walked over to the bags of coffee beans that

would have blocked the view of the safe. "Maybe it's an old employee from the previous owner."

"Maybe." I shrugged, hearing fresh voices out front.

Ian and I walked out to see Elena and her husband surveying the damage.

Elena's gaze caught mine, and I pressed my lips together in a fine line and nodded.

She obviously thought the same thing I did.

"Hey, Jaxson." I walked over to Elena's husband. "Good to see you."

"It would be nice if our family get-togethers didn't always involve some element of nefarious activity." Jaxson's dark brows rose as he laughed.

I shook my head as Sadie walked over to her sister. "Beggars can't be choosers."

"We're headed over to the police station. The officer had something he wanted to share with us," I explained quietly. "Did you want to come?"

Jaxson nodded. "Absolutely."

Sadie took a step closer. "I'll go get Melanie."

"Actually, the officer thought it might be better if

only you came with us."

Confusion fluttered through her gaze and then disappointment at the realization that she probably had been the target of this mess.

She walked over and explained to Melanie about going to the police station as we walked out of the coffee shop, feeling the chill in the air pick up.

We all piled into Ian's SUV and drove the quick few blocks to the police station. There wasn't much said as he found a place to park and we all walked into the lobby.

The smells of fresh paint and carpet permeated the air. The building was a new facility and a state-of-the-art training center for the region's search and rescue efforts.

There wasn't anyone at the front counter, but Officer Carl spotted us and came up front.

"This is Sadie's sister and brother-in-law."

Elena stuck out her hand. "Elena Volkov."

Jaxson did the same.

"I know we all have places to be, but I thought I picked something up on the security footage. It was grainy at best, but thanks to your generous donation to modernize this facility, we were able to combat the lousy footage." He waved us back as we filed down the hall into a dark room.

The soft hum of technology hung in the air as Sadie scanned the room.

Officer Carl waved toward a large screen and walked over to the AV equipment before meticulously adjusting the playback.

I glanced at Sadie, whose eyes were narrowed as she focused on the fuzzy black-and-white images in front of us.

As Officer Carl toggled the playback, he pulled up a grainy image.

It was impossible to see details of the person other than their general size and build, which didn't look to be too large.

"Now, this is what I find interesting." He pointed at what looked like the mirror I had noticed in the back room.

He zoomed in. "See this?"

"A mirror?" Elena asked.

"Yeah." Officer Carl nodded. "And this."

The pixelated image cleared to reveal the reflection of a phone in the intruder's hand.

"Looks to me that our suspect had access to the safe code." The officer glanced at Sadie and then at me.

"What does that have to do with Sadie? She was with me last night."

"Watch this."

He resumed the footage, paused it again, and managed to zoom the image to reveal a photo on the phone.

"It's Sadie," Elena whispered, craning her neck toward the screen.

"I'm going to reach out to the prior owners, get a list of previous employees, and see if we can find a connection between you and whoever broke in."

"And you've worked there for…?" Officer Carl trailed off.

"About six months. I moved here because I had started dating Zack, found an apartment, and this job kind of appeared out of the blue."

"How so?" he asked.

"I was going to give myself a month or so before I looked for something, but I went into the coffee shop one day, and Melanie was there with the old owners." Sadie laughed. "She looked completely overwhelmed and joked, asking if I needed a job, and I said sure."

"Good to know." Officer Carl turned off the screen. "I'll be in touch if I have any other questions."

We all nodded and followed the officer back out front.

I glanced at Sadie and knew there was something she didn't tell us.

Chapter Nine

Sadie

"How are you doing?" Elena asked, stretching on the chaise in Zack's living room. Jaxson was working on the phone with his brothers in another room.

"I am waiting to be able to live a normal life, free from kidnappings, break-ins, heartbreak, and general malaise."

Elena chuckled, and I felt immensely better. There was something about having my sister here that helped. I didn't feel so isolated.

But I knew none of them thought I should go

back into the coffee shop.

"Thanks for making some coffee," I told Elena, taking a sip from the mug. The smell of freshly brewed coffee filled the air.

"So, tell me what you really saw on that screen," Elena said, eying me over her own mug of coffee.

My stomach tensed, but I knew better.

"What do you mean? I saw the same things you did."

"You're not telling us something, Sadie. I can tell. I'm your sister."

The palms of my hands got sweaty as I thought back to the images. It wasn't what I saw on there. It was what I didn't.

But I didn't want to raise alarm or point fingers until I could make sure I wasn't losing my own mind.

"It's nothing. I'm just..." I sighed. "I'm exhausted. I feel like I've been looking over my shoulder for the last few weeks, and that was before Carmella even got out of jail."

Elena nodded. "Zack filled me in. It's got to be scary and probably pulls you right back to being held in that warehouse."

A shiver ran through me as I thought back to those days. The cold dampness of the floor. The constant chill in the air. The hunger and thirst.

"I'm so tired, Elena. Tired of always feeling like I'm going to do the wrong thing and wind up in a similar situation."

She nodded and didn't press. I appreciated that about my sister. She knew the answers would come and didn't push me to reveal anything before I was ready.

Zack was the same.

"How has it been being with Zack again?" she asked.

I let out a groan. "I think I'd rather talk about being kidnapped again."

"That good, huh?"

I smiled and nodded. "Actually, that's the problem. It has been good. It feels like we've never been apart. We picked up right where we left off. Things are just so easy with him. He makes me feel things I've never felt."

"Do you regret breaking up with him?" she

asked.

"I don't know. But I did it, and here we are." I shook my head slowly. "I doubt I'll ever find someone like him again. He's so level-headed, intelligent, funny, loyal."

"And extremely good-looking."

I chuckled. "And there's that. Yeah. He's extremely buff, too."

"It's okay to change your mind."

My brows shot up. "You mean with Zack?"

She nodded.

"I don't want to play games with his heart, and I'm too unstable to know which end is up."

"You're not unstable. You're working through trauma. That's not being unstable."

"It just feels like it sometimes, and my therapist pointed out that I can't ever move past trauma if I'm confronted with it every day."

"Hmm…"

I stared at my sister. "What?"

"Do you think that's realistic?"

"Which part?"

"You won't ever just forget what happened to you. But Zack was the one good thing that came out of that bad situation. That doesn't mean he's a bad reminder of the past. He was the light, the hope."

Her words hit hard.

"Listen, do you remember the men you've dated before Zack?"

I shifted uncomfortably on the couch.

"Does Wasabi Guy ring a bell?"

I chuckled, shaking my head. "It's not like I can forget Wasabi Guy. I'll never be able to get the image out of my head of him being carted out of the sushi restaurant on a stretcher."

Elena laughed. "Nothing like dating in the city."

"He seemed so worldly and cultured, and the next thing I know, he's spooning in wasabi like it's guacamole—and bam. Turned a million shades of a strawberry. Jerry was his name. He never returned my calls either."

"But would you have wanted him to?"

I laughed, feeling immensely better being with my sister.

"And don't forget how your first boyfriend became obsessed with you." Elena rolled her eyes. "He never knew when to leave you alone. Remember how Dad had to step in?"

A chill instantly fell across my skin.

"Don't remind me." I looked up at my sister, wondering if I should tell her what had happened a few weeks ago. It would be safe with her, and she probably wouldn't overreact. Although, with everything going on with Carmella, that wasn't a guarantee.

And I needed to tell someone.

I pushed the sick feeling aside. "Yeah. He had some issues."

Zack cleared his throat, and my eyes met his as he stood in the living room.

"Wasabi Guy?" A smile touched Zack's mouth, and I couldn't help but feel the familiar charge from him. "First boyfriend drama. What a great time to enter the room."

"I'm going to check on Jaxson," Elena said, hopping up from the chaise with her coffee and a big smile.

As she left, Zack slowly walked toward me.

"I've got some good news." He smiled wider, making me feel like the luckiest woman in the world. It was such a genuine thing for him.

"Lay it on me. I'd love to hear some." I stretched my arms toward the ceiling and yawned.

"I bored you already?"

I laughed, noticing a glimmer of hope behind his gaze.

And it killed me. I knew what he wanted, but I just couldn't give it to him.

"That's one thing about you. You're never boring," I assured him. "So let me have some good news."

"I'm making my infamous carbonara tonight for everyone." He smiled, and I grinned. "And Officer Carl thinks it might be an ex-employee from the previous owners."

I chuckled as he took a seat next to me on the couch. Our bodies were a few inches apart, but I could feel the heat from him rolling over to me.

I'd spent many a night curled against Zack on this

couch. The thought made my stomach squeeze with regret.

He slowly brushed a piece of hair from my forehead.

"What about the photo of me?" I asked.

"We don't know yet." He didn't take his eyes off mine. "But we'll know more as soon as he does."

I nodded, silently wishing I could tell him everything that had happened since I broke up with him, but he was already doing more than enough, and I didn't need him to go nuclear.

There were some things I needed to do on my own.

He turned to see me better on the couch as I propped my elbows on my knees, curling into a ball of nerves.

"I won't bite. I promise," he said, gently patting my knee.

It felt good.

"Do you ever make mistakes? Like, epic mistakes?" I asked Zack.

He kicked out his legs and folded his hands

behind the back of his head, stretching. "No. At this point in my life, I'm pretty much perfection." He rolled his eyes and shook his head. "Of course, I make mistakes. Daily, if not hourly. Why do you ask?"

I straightened and pushed my feet toward his lap. "I just feel like I've made a lot of mistakes throughout my life, and it's all just led me to this moment."

Zack's expression fell, and he pulled my feet closer to him, squeezing them through my pink fuzzy socks.

"You did absolutely nothing to deserve this. You didn't bring any of this on yourself. You're dealing with some money-hungry, power-hungry individuals embedded in a web far larger than any of us realized. It wasn't like you made a mistake and everything like this tumbled down on you."

"No. I know. I just feel like I've made some mistakes along the way."

"No more than most people," he said softly. "I wish you'd quit blaming yourself, Sadie."

I knew he meant it. He always did. He always made me feel worthy and heard.

So why did I value the trauma more than the healing? Why did I break up with him?

Zack's eyes locked on mine as I tucked my feet underneath me and scooted closer to him. It felt like all the air in the room had been sucked out, and I was floating in a tipsy euphoria as his eyes lowered to my lips.

Without a second thought, I looked into his hazel eyes, the flecks of gold intensifying as he bit his bottom lip and moved his arms around my waist, waiting for my permission.

I stared at him, wanting to be kissed.

"I don't want to play with your heart, Zack," I whispered, feeling the desire race between us.

"I'm a big boy. I can handle a kiss, Sadie." The fire in his gaze scorched my soul.

I needed this from him.

I wanted to feel safe again.

The world stilled around us as the longing intensified in Zack's gaze. The noise of Elena and Jaxson speaking in the other room faded into a low hum. Zack's eyes stayed on mine as he searched for some sort of soundless permission in a silent and crazy conversation that only we understood.

My pulse quickened as I thought about all the times I had wanted to be held by Zack this last month, all the times I wanted to be kissed by him. But I had chased him away.

Zack reached out and brushed a stray hair from my cheek, but his fingers lingered on the curve of my jaw before trailing down my neck. A shiver of anticipation ran through me from the gentle touch of his hand.

I took a slow, shaky breath as desire filled every cell in my body. My eyes fell to his lips in a silent permission. Zack nodded ever so slightly and leaned in, cupping my chin with his fingers.

Zack slid his hands behind me, scooping me into him as his lips fleetingly brushed against mine. My breath hitched from the heat of our lips connecting as he waited for my permission.

I wriggled my body in a quiet invitation as his mouth met mine, hungrier the second time. His kiss deepened, becoming more passionate with each passing moment. I parted my lips, mingling our breaths and shared longing.

It was as if time were suspended and nothing else mattered as his tongue playfully tasted me, kissing me with more emotion than I'd ever felt. He ran his hands up my spine as a wave of goosebumps cascaded along my skin.

He tasted so good, so familiar.

The comfort and security I felt in his arms brought me right back to that first day I'd met him.

In the warehouse.

I breathed in quickly and opened my eyes as Zack's mouth parted from mine.

"I'm so sorry, Sadie. I thought…"

"Don't apologize. I wanted it. I still want it."

He nodded slowly as I looped my arms around his neck and scooted all the way onto his lap.

My mouth touched down on his once more, and I knew this would be the last kiss we shared.

Chapter Ten

Zack

I should be elated about the kiss I shared with Sadie, but I knew there was a meaning behind it that I didn't understand. I glanced over at my brother, who'd just received confirmation that Carmela was still on the East Coast.

Jaxson, Elena, and Sadie all bundled up and took a walk out back. I didn't like the idea, but her threat was theoretically thousands of miles away, and Jaxson could certainly take care of anyone who surprised them.

And it gave me a chance to speak with my

brother. "I think Sadie's hiding something."

"You think she's seeing someone?"

My expression fell. I hadn't even considered that.

"Oh. My bad." Ian laughed. "I'm sure that's not it. I thought maybe…"

"Thanks for that." I shook my head and laughed. "I hadn't really given that a thought, but I guess considering she broke up with me over a month ago, it could be the cause."

Ian laughed nervously and shook his head. "Nah. I doubt it. So, what's up? What makes you think she's keeping something from you?"

"I can't put my finger on it, but there's like half-thoughts spilling out of her mouth, interrupted guesses, partial backtracks. It's all just… unlike her."

"You don't think she had something to do with the break-in, do you?"

I couldn't hide the shock. "Not even a little bit. She was here at the house, and that wasn't the direction in the conversation I was headed at all."

"Officer Carl asked me," he confessed. "I told him she was sleeping at your house, and he dropped it."

I nodded, wishing I'd kept things to myself. Ian didn't know Sadie like I did or he never would have asked that question, and it didn't make me feel great that Officer Carl had questioned Sadie's whereabouts either.

"All I'm saying is I know something isn't right, and I don't believe it only concerns Carmella." I walked over to the window in my office. Even though it was only October, a light dusting of snow coated the naked tree limbs outside. It would probably melt by tomorrow, but it was a swift reminder that winter was coming.

"Stay focused on the problem at hand. Don't go trying to make more."

I clenched my jaw. "I'm not, but I've been in this business long enough to know when something isn't right." I spun around from the window and faced my brother. "Our parents taught us how important our instincts were. I don't know why you're suddenly discounting those."

My security system buzzed, and I glanced at the video by the front gate. I squinted my eyes before recognizing the person.

I glanced at my brother as the driver rolled down

her window and pressed the button.

"It's Melanie," I told my brother, who suddenly lit up.

"Something you want to mention about the barista?" I joked.

My brother's expression returned to stone. "Listen, I know what Mom and Dad taught us, but they also ensured that we took personal feelings out of our equations. The problem here is that your equation is riddled with personal factors." He shook his head. "You're still in love with her. You can't separate that out."

I picked up the photograph of my parents propped on my desk and sighed.

"They spent their entire lives protecting us, and the moment they took a break, they were gone."

Ian studied me. "Those two things aren't parallel."

"If they hadn't let their guard down, they'd still be here. I'm not letting my guard down."

Ian pushed his fingers through his hair and groaned.

"We can't go back and change the past, just like we can't know what the future holds. But Mom and Dad wouldn't want you putting yourself in danger because you can't separate your feelings for this girl."

"She's not just some girl, Ian."

The doorbell chimed, and I shook my head. "We'll discuss it later."

"Absolutely."

I made my way to the door with Ian behind me.

The moment I swung it open, Ian seemed extra animated, nearly jumping in front of me to invite Melanie in.

"I didn't mean to barge in. I just wanted to see how Sadie was doing, and I couldn't reach her on the phone. I hope I'm not intruding."

"Not—"

Ian shook his head, interrupting me. "Not at all."

I hid my smile and gestured down the hall with my brother and Melanie behind me. When I reached the kitchen, Sadie and her family were coming back inside.

Sadie spotted Melanie immediately and smiled while Elena beelined to the coffee pot.

"I'm so glad to see you," Melanie said, touching her chest. "You didn't answer your messages, so I got worried… you know, with everything going on."

Sadie looked truly touched and nodded. "I'm totally fine. Just left my phone in my bedroom to charge."

Melanie laughed and glanced over at me. "Sorry. I guess I've officially turned into a worrywart. I just don't want anything to happen to you."

Elena walked over with a mug of coffee and handed it to Melanie. "The more, the merrier. My sister needs as many eyes on her as possible. She's a handful."

"I am merely a magnet for chaos." Sadie scowled and poured herself her own cup of coffee. "I think that's what my therapist told me."

I shook my head. "I'm just putting this out there, but have you considered getting a new one? Your therapist doesn't seem very nice."

Sadie snickered. "She's really good, and you just don't like her because of some of her advice."

I laughed, nodding. "Yeah. Precisely."

Sadie traded a knowing look with her sister, and

I knew to tone it down. I might have said it all with a laugh, but I didn't feel light about it at all.

"You have perfect timing," I told Melanie. "I was just about to start dinner. You're welcome to stay."

Melanie's cheeks reddened. "Oh, I don't want to intrude."

Sadie reached for her and clutched her hands. "Stay. I insist."

Melanie looked over at me, and I nodded. "We have plenty of food. Don't make it a wasted trip."

She nodded. "Okay, then. Count me in."

Several minutes passed as I was cooking dinner, and I noticed Melanie over with Elena, Jaxson, and Ian, but I didn't see Sadie.

I glanced back at Melanie and noticed her looking around the family room and not really paying attention to what my brother was saying.

Poor guy.

If that was who he had his sights on, it might not pan out for him.

"Smells delicious," Sadie said, coming up behind me.

"Thanks." I reached for the tongs and noticed Sadie scowling at her phone.

"What's up?"

Sadie's eyes connected with mine, and she shrugged. "Nothing."

"It looks like something."

"Maybe later," she whispered as I mixed the pasta.

I nodded before pulling out the garlic bread.

"I'll go set the table," Sadie said, smiling.

It suddenly felt like old times. Watching her grab the silverware and wander over to the table, my chest tightened at the memory, and the longing gripped me as emotion ran deep.

Her laughter tickled the air, and the desire to start fresh with her stirred.

I glanced at Sadie, and her beauty caught me off guard. Even with all the struggles and the inner turmoil she was going through, she managed to appear carefree and happy.

Since she'd broken up with me, I still found myself conjuring up scenarios where I'd accidentally bump into her around town or how I'd somehow win her back, proving to her that I didn't need to be a reminder of that awful experience.

I shook my head at the irony as I brought the bowl of pasta over.

Here Sadie was, in my house, because of the very event that brought us together.

"What's up?" she asked, bringing over the garlic bread.

Everyone found a seat at the table, and our eyes locked on one another. It was like nobody else existed in our small world.

I wanted to tell her how much I loved her. How we could make this work after everything was over. How much I wanted to start over.

As the tension grew thicker, she blinked, looking away.

I knew she felt every bit of the desire and longing building up between us.

"This looks fabulous," Melanie hummed as Sadie patted her shoulders.

"Zack is the best chef in town." Sadie smiled,

sneaking another look at me.

I shrugged. "I try. Anyone care for some wine?"

Before Jax sat down, he nodded and walked into the kitchen. "Tell me where it is, and I'll do the honors. You have a seat. You've done plenty for our family."

"I wish I could do more," I said, shaking my head. "In the fridge."

"Me too. I feel so helpless," Melanie said softly as Sadie took a seat between her and her sister.

"We're all doing the best we can," Elena said, smiling at Melanie, "And we'll come out of this stronger as a family and ready for whatever the world has to hand us."

Sadie groaned. "Honestly, I think this is all I want the world to hand me. I'm pretty much beat."

Melanie nodded. "I can understand that." She pressed her lips into a thin line as Jaxson opened a bottle of Pinot Grigio. Sadie had already placed the wine glasses for everyone at the table.

Sadie helped plate everyone's food as silence settled over the table with people eating pasta, drinking wine, and enjoying the evening.

Except it was anything but normal.

"My brothers have been keeping tabs on Carmella, and she is still very much planted in New York."

Relief dashed through Sadie's expression. "That's good news."

I nodded in agreement. I'd spoken briefly with Jaxson about the items left in Sadie's apartment, and we both agreed it wasn't a coincidence.

But with Melanie here, it didn't seem the place to bring up that topic again.

"I've read as much as I could about the incident," Melanie said, looking at Sadie. "But I don't know the why of it. How did you become the target?"

Elena let out a deep breath as Sadie stared at her plate. I wanted to reach over and pull her into me, shield her from the nightmare that had become her life.

Sadie straightened in her seat and brought her gaze to Melanie's. "My sister wrote a crime blog, and she was narrowing in on some stuff that implicated some high-ranking politicians. So, to silence my sister, they targeted me."

"Wow. I'm so sorry." Melanie took a sip of wine. "That's just unbelievable."

"In every sense of the word," I said, watching Sadie.

She went back to eating, and I wondered what made Melanie ask that so point blankly when she'd been so careful to tiptoe around Sadie before.

Unless she was blaming Sadie for what happened at her shop.

But that didn't seem like Melanie's usual character.

"Well, I'm keeping the coffee shop closed for a few days while we put in a security system and just to kind of regroup."

Sadie smiled sympathetically. "Take as much time as you need."

"Yeah. That's what my parents said, too." She chuckled. "This just gave them another reason to have me come back to live in the town I grew up in. So, I can't even imagine what you've gone through."

Sadie froze, and I could tell that something had triggered her.

I cleared my throat. "The good news is that Carmella should be put away again soon, and we can put that behind us."

Sadie nodded as she ate, but her eyes connected with mine, and I knew these feelings I still had for Sadie weren't simple, and neither were the ones she felt for me.

But before I could worry about any of that, I needed to make the world safe again for her, even if that meant letting go of her in the process.

Maybe the therapist was right.

Chapter Eleven

Sadie

I knew I was fully at the point of being paranoid. I completely recognized that, but I also knew that Melanie's texts had never reached me.

And with today's cell service, that was highly unlikely. Even in our small mountain town, we didn't have many dead patches.

But she also didn't have any reason to lie about it, so that's why I knew I was being paranoid.

Melanie left shortly after dinner, and the rest of us watched a movie before we all headed to bed. I'd thought about telling Zack about not receiving her text last night, but I just didn't have it in me to stay up for another two hours rehashing it.

But this morning, it was on top of my mind the second I woke up, and I knew I needed to tell him.

I rolled over, feeling the softness of the sheets on my arms before willing myself to uncover and grab my phone.

Sitting up in bed, I reached for my robe and wandered over to where I'd plugged my phone in last night.

There were six messages from Melanie, all asking if I was alright. I opened them up and realized these must have been the texts she'd been talking about. I chuckled to myself, realizing I really had embraced paranoia.

So, that was great.

It made me feel much better, like I could breathe deeply again.

I opened up my favorite social media app, expecting to see some great puppy pics or someone's great dinner from last night, but I sucked in a sharp breath when I saw another message from my old boyfriend in my social media inbox.

His first one left me unsettled several weeks ago, but I promised myself that since I hadn't heard from him anymore, it was just him checking up on me. That maybe he'd grown as a person, fallen in love with someone else, and moved on.

It had been a simple message.

Hope all is well with you in your mountain town, my little seashell. We should catch up sometime.

~Tim

But I couldn't dismiss the fact that, at that time, I'd started to feel like someone was watching me.

I also never messaged him back because I knew better than to encourage someone who'd had that behavior in the past. It had literally taken my dad to step in when I tried to end things with Tim.

Another thing I had to do was remind myself that it was obvious I'd moved to my mountain town because of the profile images I'd shared, not because he was stalking me again.

A cold breeze shot through me, but the air in my room was absolutely still. I didn't want to open the message, but I knew I had to.

But as I stared at his name, the chill went deeper.

The memories that had long turned into shadows of my mind resurfaced, and my hands trembled.

Could he be involved with the coffee shop?

I moved the tip of my finger to the inbox, hovering over his name, and clicked it.

Ah, I see you think you're better than me. Too good to answer a message from an old boyfriend, my little seashell? Too famous from being kidnapped back home? You're lucky it wasn't me who'd done that to you. Your superhero of a boyfriend would never have found you.

The first message, there had been no overt threats, but this one…

I closed the app and set down my phone, trying to remind myself to stay calm with a few deep breaths.

This didn't mean he was here. He could just be bored.

He always liked to torment me, leaving me little reminders and vague notes.

No. I had enough going on. I wasn't going to let this guy get underneath me. He probably knew Carmella was out on a technicality and wanted to freak me out.

As I convinced myself that my ex was harmless, I walked to the bathroom and started the shower. Feeling the steam coat my body and lungs relaxed my muscles as I moved into the shower.

I was getting paranoid. My first boyfriend was all bark, no bite.

I had more significant issues to worry about. I needed to focus on remaining calm and rational while the prosecutor worked on getting Carmella behind bars again.

She was a threat.

My old boyfriend was a nuisance.

As I worked the suds from my hair, I took another deep breath and let it out slowly, staring at the droplets cascading down the glass.

Just one step at a time.

I turned off the water, dried off, and quickly pulled some clothes on before going to the kitchen, where I could hear Zack, Jaxson, and Elena chatting.

The sound instantly calmed me.

I was here with friends and family. Everything was fine.

I would be okay.

I was okay.

When I walked into the kitchen, they all turned to see me as Zack held up the coffee pot.

"Not as good as what you make, but would you like some?" His eyes drifted to mine as I forced myself to make it look like everything was fine.

"I'd love some." I hugged my sister, and she tapped my hand and squeezed it.

"Did you sleep okay?" she asked.

"I actually did."

She nodded, taking in my expression.

The two people who could read me better than most happened to be standing in this kitchen, my sister and my ex.

But I didn't want to throw this ridiculous message into the mix.

My phone rang, and I jumped just as Zack handed me the cup of coffee, spilling a few drops onto the counter.

His eyes narrowed on mine as Elena grabbed a towel to wipe up the coffee.

I glanced at the phone. "It's the prosecutor."

Zack stilled as I put the call on speakerphone.

"Hello?" My words were nearly a whisper.

Hi, Sadie. This is Jack. I hope you're doing well.

"I'd be better if Carmella were behind bars."

He sighed. *Well, that's precisely what I'm calling about. Her attorney is interested in a plea deal.*

My stomach sank, but I continued.

"So, she's not going to jail?" My voice trembled.

No, she'd still be doing jail time. I didn't like their initial offer, but I did send them one that would be fair and—

I let out a deep breath, but I still felt like I wanted to explode.

"No, being fair is if she were still in jail, awaiting her trial for attempted murder. This isn't fair," I told him.

You're right, Sadie. I misspoke, but I do have to consider many factors when deciding what cases to take to trial.

I shook my head. "She would be proven

guilty."

Juries can be surprising.

I clenched my fists, leaning against the counter for strength. I refused to look at Zack.

"What are you offering them?"

Four years in prison, three years probation. I think the judge will sign off on it.

It felt like the world was spinning around me. The walls felt like they were closing in as I stared at the moving ceiling. None of this made sense.

Zack came up behind me, looping his arm around me, holding me tight as I brought my gaze back down to the phone.

Her defense lawyer only wanted two years of jail time with one year of probation.

I froze for a brief second.

Zack slowly rubbed my back, trying to soothe me.

But there was no making me feel better.

I turned to look at Zack and nodded.

"Fine."

The good news is that she'll return to jail by the weekend. The judge will sign off quickly.

I nodded, even though he couldn't see. "Well, thanks for letting me know."

I'm sorry we couldn't get her in for what we'd originally planned.

I sighed. "Me too."

And then I hung up the phone.

It was like my life was in slow motion. Every second felt like an hour as I stared at the counter while Zack rubbed my back.

"I know this isn't what you wanted."

I slowly raised my arms, wrapping them around myself and shaking my head. "Not at all."

"What can I do? How can I make this better?"

I steadied my breathing.

"I don't know. Just... thank you for being here."

"I'll always be here for you, Sadie."

I would have four years of peace. I wouldn't have to relive everything over again for a trial. I could do this. I could stay strong, make a plan, disappear...

"That will give you enough time to do what you'd planned."

I shook my head, staring at him blankly. "What did I plan?"

"You know, you'd mentioned wanting to create a therapy space with animals for trauma victims."

I laughed, feeling bitterness overtake me. "Yeah. Right. That."

"Don't do this, Sadie. Don't let Carmella get you

down. Don't give her that power."

I looked into his beautiful eyes and shook my head. "You're right. I know you're right, but right now, all I want to do is fly away and hide and just be done with this." A shiver ran through me.

Zack put both of his large hands on my shoulders and rubbed my arms up and down.

Elena laughed nervously. "We'd all miss you too much."

Jaxson glanced at Zack as if to ask him something private, which only annoyed me more.

"What? What's the secret look about?" I stepped away. "Are you thinking about hiding me somewhere?"

Zack's lip curled slightly, and he shook his head. "No. We wouldn't dream of doing that, Sadie."

But the way Zack's expression darkened made me wonder what Jaxson and he had spoken about. I glanced at my sister, but she didn't appear to have any insight either.

With everything that just went on, I almost forgot about the earlier message from my first boyfriend.

Zack poured himself another cup of coffee, and I

was tempted to dismiss the message from Tim.

"So, Carmella is still on the East Coast." I drew a breath and glanced at Jaxson, who had people watching her.

He nodded, pushing his thumb along his jawline. "Yeah. I got confirmation thirty minutes ago."

I nodded, feeling my shoulders drop. "Well, I might have an idea who's been leaving things in my apartment."

Zack's gaze snapped to me as Elena closed the gap between us.

"Who?"

I bit my lip and shook my head, feeling absolutely ridiculous. How did I attract this kind of problem? These kinds of people?

"My ex-boyfriend."

Jaxson scowled and looked at Zack, and I laughed as he put both hands in the air.

"No, I mean from a long time ago."

Elena cocked her head slightly as her eyes met mine. "Are you talking about your first boyfriend?"

I pushed my lips into a thin line and nodded.

"Yeah. I got a message from him several weeks ago that seemed rather harmless and unassuming, and I didn't answer. I knew Dad would kill me if I opened that door again."

Elena nodded. "Indeed."

"And then this morning, I woke up to a new message, and this time it was… threatening."

Elena groaned and looked up at the ceiling as Jaxson and Zack traded another look.

"Why do I think there's a history here we should know about?" Jaxson asked as Zack walked over.

I glanced at the stool near the island and took a seat. "My very first boyfriend out of high school turned very possessive. So much so that our dad had to get involved and put a stop to things."

"Okay. I don't like where this is going." Zack leaned over the island, propping his elbows on the granite, which made his forearms bulge.

I thought about the scrawny, menacing kid I'd left behind so many years ago and knew there was no competition between the two. I held in a wry smile and stared at Zack.

"Well, he did all kinds of creepy things back then." I looked at my sister. "Was I about twenty when he finally left me alone?"

She nodded. "Something like that."

"What kind of creepy things?" Zack asked.

"Well, he'd just always show up wherever I was, and he'd leave intimidating notes and little mementos. He always called me his little seashell, so he'd leave shells around."

"And all it took was your dad talking to him to get him to stop?"

I nodded. "My dad told Tim that we'd be going to the authorities, and since Tim wanted to be an attorney, I suppose he realized that wouldn't be a great idea. Although, I don't think he ever went to law school. He left me alone after that."

"Until now."

I nodded, folding my arms across my chest. The tightness underneath my breastbone had returned, and taking deep breaths felt like I was running a marathon.

"Can I see the messages?" Zack asked.

I nodded as Elena reached for my phone and

handed it to him.

"Do you mind if I take it into my office?"

I laughed. "I have nothing to hide. No hot dates tonight or anything."

A glimmer of relief flashed in Zack's eyes, but I wasn't sure for what, in particular.

Jaxson followed Zack out of the kitchen as Elena plopped down on the stool beside me. She reached for my hand and squeezed it.

"Things will get back to normal someday, Sadie. I promise."

I laughed and shook my head, taking a sip of coffee. "You know better than to make promises you can't keep."

"Okay. How about the *new* normal?" The kindness in her eyes dropped a veil of comfort over me that I desperately needed.

"Just promise me that you'll do what Zack says. I know you two aren't dating, even though he wishes with every part of his being that you were, but please do what he says. He protects people for a living."

I frowned. "What makes you think I wouldn't do

what he says?"

She laughed, tilting her head. "Uh, because you've never liked being told what to do."

I chuckled, knowing my sister knew me too well.

"Did you catch any of the looks between the boys? Do you know what they're up to?"

Elena shook her head. "Not a clue."

The murmurs from down the hall drifted into the kitchen, but I couldn't understand what they were saying.

But for the first time in a long time, it felt amazing to give up control and trust that things would work out.

Even if I didn't believe that deep in my heart.

Even if I knew I might need to spend my life running.

Chapter Twelve

Zack

"This is not good." I shook my head, feeling my pulse pound between my ears.

Jaxson paced in front of me. "Not good at all."

My brother was on his way over, and I had so much chaotic energy bottling up that I needed to stay away from Sadie. It felt like I wanted to simultaneously pummel her jerk of an ex while dropping Carmella into the ocean, and she didn't need to see that side of me.

Sadie needed a cool, calm, and collected protector. Not the one letting his emotions guide his every move.

"If you look at the guy, it shouldn't be much of a challenge." Jaxson's eyes met mine.

I nodded. "True."

Jaxson laughed, shaking his head as he took a seat. "But I know you guys do it the right way, and we…"

I kept my gaze on his. "You have your own methods."

And suddenly, I wasn't so averse to them.

"That we do."

"So, by the looks of it, Tim Venson is living in North Carolina." I walked over to my laptop and clicked on his profile. He looked like a weasel.

But what concerned me more was that he also looked like he had a fulfilling life.

So why focus on Sadie?

I scratched my chin and shook my head.

Ian walked into the office and grinned the moment he saw Jaxson. "You two look like you're ready to break some bones."

I laughed and gave my brother a quick hug. "It's

been one hell of a morning. First, Sadie finds out the case isn't going to trial because of a plea deal, and then Sadie tells us she's been getting contacted by her stalker boyfriend."

Ian whistled and shook his head. "You certainly know how to pick 'em."

"Well, she didn't pick me back, so there's…"

Sadie appeared behind Ian, and her eyes widened.

Shit. She heard.

I played it off and turned my attention to my brother, but I noticed Sadie's gaze lingered.

"My brother is going to do some digging on your ex, and we'll see if we can place him here. I'm going to talk with Officer Carl, too, and keep him in the loop. It's a small town. We'll be able to spot someone out of the ordinary."

She nodded, rocking back on her heels. "I feel like I need a walk. I have a therapy session online in like an hour, so maybe before it?"

"Okay," I said, glancing at Jaxson. "Did you want Jaxson and Elena to accompany you?"

Her expression fell. "So, you think my ex could actually be here? That I can't just go outside for a walk?"

My eyes stayed on hers as dread crept through me. I knew what she meant. Would she ever be through with all the hiding and looking over her shoulder? But I couldn't, in good faith, tell her to hike freely through the woods.

She just looked at me and waited. "I think it's a high possibility that your ex was here, but I don't know if he is. We won't know that for a bit."

Ian returned her phone, and she slipped it into her pocket.

Sadie drew in a slow breath and let it out equally as deliberately. "I'd like you to walk with me, if that's okay."

My heart spun on its axis. Of course, it was okay. I wanted nothing more than to spend all my time with Sadie.

Over the last six months, she'd become my constant companion when I was here. I loved just being with her, listening to her laugh or the way she loved to rib me about my workout routine—just everything.

I loved everything about Sadie.

I clutched my hands together and squeezed them as I nodded. "Yup. Fine, that sounds good. I'll meet you at the front door in about five minutes."

A brightness darted through her beautiful eyes, and I felt my throat clench at the thought of not having her.

But I knew this was temporary. When Carmella was back behind bars and we figured out what was going on with her ex, she'd be gone.

My body turned as still as a boulder as I watched her head down the hallway, and all I could think about was how much I felt every crack running through my stone exterior. I missed her, and she was right in front of me.

"You okay, bud?" my brother asked sympathetically.

I nodded. "Yeah. I'm fine. I have to get used to us not being an us."

"Yeah." Ian walked over to my laptop and started typing. "I'll do some more research while you're out with Sadie. Maybe she can give you some more clues about the guy she used to date."

"Whatever we find out, I think it's safe to say we need to teach this guy a lesson." Jaxson's low growl of a laugh made me smile.

"You're about as Alpha as they come, aren't ya?"

He grinned. "I never really thought about it, but I'm not the one with muscles bursting the seams of my shirts."

I laughed and shook my head. "At least we all still have our sense of humor."

Making my way down the hall to the mudroom, I saw Elena giving Sadie a big hug. Her sister's eyes connected with mine, and I quickly nodded in understanding.

No matter how you analyzed what was happening with Sadie, it wasn't fair. There was nothing she did to bring any of this to herself. All Carmella had wanted was to get back at Elena and the Volkov brothers. Sadie was just an innocent pawn in everything. And this guy who's sending the threatening notes sounded like nothing more than a punk who needed to be put in his place.

The problem was that in my line of work, I saw many of these punks create a lot of havoc.

But not to my Sadie.

I clenched my fists as I grabbed a jacket from the mudroom and slid my arms through the sleeves as I thought about what I'd like to do to this ex of hers.

Who did he think he was?

I shook the thought from my head. I'd always prided myself on being on the right side of the law. As a business, we ensured that we'd uphold the law and protect our clients the right way.

But I didn't care about any of that.

I just wanted peace for Sadie.

She deserved that.

Jaxson offered something earlier and I laughed it off, but the more I thought about what he and his brothers could do, I wondered...

They knew how to make problems disappear.

I closed my eyes and let the air escape my lungs. I had to get a grip. I knew what I stood for. I could solve this problem like I solved all the rest.

And I'd be there for Sadie.

I stepped out of the mudroom and saw Sadie all bundled up, looking as cute as ever in her pink goose-down jacket that almost ate her up. Her matching pink gloves and knit hat made me think about how much fun we had here when she first arrived. It was in April, and the last mountain snow had peppered everything, giving her just enough powder to make snow angels. And before I knew it, we were gently wrestling in the freezing snow, kissing and...

"I'm ready. Are you?" Sadie asked, pulling me out of Memory Lane.

Thankfully.

She moved against the wall and smiled, catching my gaze. "What's that goofy look for?"

"Honest answer?" I asked.

"Always."

"I was thinking about the first time you dressed like a pink marshmallow when you arrived."

Her cheeks flushed. "Oh, yeah. That was fun."

I nodded. "It always is with you."

Sadie's expression fell slightly. "And then you had to leave for three weeks."

It was like a piece of dynamite exploded in my heart.

She was right. I always had to leave.

I took a step closer, brushing my finger along her cheek. "I wish my life were different, Sadie. I actually—"

Sadie shook her head, cutting me off. "Sorry. I didn't mean it like that. I can't expect you to give up what you love."

"It's not like that. I've come to realize—"

She stood on her toes and placed a quick kiss on my cheek to stop me. "Let's just be grateful for the amazing time we had together. I regret nothing, and the same should go for you."

There was so much I'd wanted to tell Sadie. There were so many plans that my brother and I had discussed that involved the evolution of the company and my role… and then it was too late.

She held out her gloved hand. "Ready?"

"Absolutely. Let's get you some fresh air."

As we made our way outside, the chill in the air reminded me why I loved living in the mountains year-round.

Granite Peak was a fantastic place to recharge after a high-intensity job. Pretty much everyone left everyone alone, and the tourists generally only added a bit of liveliness during the ski, leaf, and ATV seasons.

It was the solitude I'd craved growing up in such a vigorous family. I was so grateful for my parents and the life they'd given us and the knowledge they'd handed over to us through the years. I'd just never expected the reason behind their cautious living to be so...

Horrendous.

"It's so pretty with all the leaves changing," she said quietly, her hand still in mine as she looked up to see the towering maples glowing fiery reds, oranges, and yellows. "The East Coast always gets the credit for leaves, but this is beautiful."

I nodded, taking it all in through Sadie's eyes.

"Are you sure you have to leave?"

I regretted the words as soon as I let them out. I wasn't trying to make her stay for me. I just wanted her to be sure she wanted to leave for her.

Sadie's smile turned up higher on the corner as

her gaze met mine, and the thought settled on me that maybe she'd reconsidered.

"We've shared a lot of amazing times, Zack, but I feel like I'm just a ball of drama, and you deal with enough of that in your day job."

"That's not how I feel, though, Sadie." We kept walking down a gravel path leading into the woods on my property.

She shrugged and sucked in a deep breath. "I know. But it's just not the right time."

I shook my head but stayed quiet as we walked deeper into the woods.

"Of course, Elena told my parents about Tim." She glanced over at me. "So, they're completely panicked, and my dad is kicking himself for never reporting him to the authorities."

I shook my head. "No one could have predicted that he'd just lie in waiting."

"Yeah. I almost forgot about him, to be honest."

I laughed. "Don't let him hear that. That will only make the little man more onery."

She slowed and pushed her hands into her puffy

pink coat pockets. "Do you think it's crazy that I want to surround myself with people who are dealing with trauma?" Sadie scanned the leaf-littered forest floor and brought her eyes to mine.

"No. I don't think it's unbelievable at all. I think it will probably bring comfort."

"There are days like today when I feel like I'm just a sucker. Like I don't see things coming, and then I fall for life's tricks."

She kicked some muddy leaves with her boot and shrugged. "I don't know. I'm just a hot mess, Zack. And I know you know it. You deal with high-profile celebrities and politicians who have their act together, and then there's me."

I tipped her chin up with my thumb until she brought her gaze to mine.

"Sadie, you've dealt with more than any of these people have dealt with. Most of my days are filled with perceived threats. You've been kidnapped. You've faced death straight on. I've never for a minute thought you were a hot mess. But just for the record, if you were the definition of a hot mess, you certainly make it look sexy."

She chuckled. "That's what is so amazing about you, Mr. Parker. You always make me feel worthy. Like what I have to say matters."

Shock spread through me.

"Of course, it matters. Who ever said it didn't?"

"Well, come to think of it... Tim. He'd always belittle what I said or how I felt. He'd made me feel so small, and at that age, you know, a girl listens to what a boyfriend says. I remember one time I'd gotten a 3.9 on a paper instead of a 4.0, but I was so relieved because I'd spent the night before the paper was due out with him and thought I'd bomb." She swayed back and forth at the memory. "And all he said was that he thought I was smarter than that."

"Wow."

"Yeah. He'd constantly tell me I was too fat or didn't have enough muscle or definition in my abs or whatever. I mean, now if I guy told me that—"

"They'd leave in a neck brace." I chuckled.

"Exactly. But he just knew how to push my buttons. If I were out with my friends or Elena, he'd message me nonstop, belittle what I was doing, tell me I'd never make anything of myself." She let out a sigh. "But now, I feel like maybe he's right. I don't even know what I want to do any longer. I mean, owning a therapy ranch is a dream, not a reality."

"It can be a reality, Sadie. I can help you make it happen."

She nodded and took a deep breath as she looked away.

Rage flooded my veins. That man would pay.

One way or another.

My way or Jaxson's.

Tim Venson would never have a chance to destroy Sadie's spirit again.

Chapter Thirteen

Sadie

"I know you've mentioned your parents worked for the government, and that was why you got into this line of work, but we never went that deep with it," I said softly, looking up at Zack.

He was so beautifully handsome. It was like I was staring at a retired linebacker turned personal security guard. But then, when you got lucky enough to peel back the layers, his heart and soul managed to outshine his good looks and create a desire I couldn't ignore.

Even now.

Zack shifted his weight, the leaves crunching underfoot as he took a deep breath. A puff of air drifted away as he nodded.

"True. I've done a pretty good job of avoiding that topic." He smiled and tilted his head as he studied me.

There was something so natural and stunning about this moment as we stood quietly in the woods, recognizing that we had managed to hold tight the secrets among us.

"Are you getting cold?" he asked.

I wiggled my gloved finger. "Nice try. I like being outside, and it's not that cold. We go in there, and I won't hear about your parents."

"I just don't know that it will bring anything to our relationship or how you see me, especially since..." His words were brutally recognizable. I'd asked the same question a million different ways, and I still didn't feel like I knew the whole truth.

And now, what leg did I have to stand on to ask for his truth? I broke up with him.

"Since we aren't together?" I continued for him.

He nodded, glancing back toward the house's silhouette through the trees.

"Yeah, but it doesn't mean I stopped caring about you." I shook my head. "I'm just curious how you can be so tender and compassionate to me and the ones you love while you do something so... aggressive for work."

Zack took a step toward me and closed the gap slightly. "They are two separate worlds, Sadie. I don't bring home my work, and I don't bring home to my work. I can't. It would be too dangerous."

"Then what about this situation? How do you explain this?"

He'd become used to hiding his reactions from me recently, and I could tell he was trying to do it again.

"Life isn't always black and white. I'm doing my job, and it just happens to be for someone I care a lot about."

"Does that make it harder?"

He was quiet for a few seconds. "It makes me realize how much I lost when you left me. I shouldn't have taken you for granted. I should have made changes to make you more comfortable. Now, I'm paying the price and doing what I can to make you safe."

His words beat ferociously through me. With each pulse, it felt like I was reopening the wounds of what we had and never could have again.

But I couldn't deny that when I was with him, I felt safest.

"My parents worked for the State Department." He cleared his throat. "They were stationed overseas for many years and didn't make friends. When my mom became pregnant with my brother, they moved back to the States. But they were always looking over their shoulders."

Of all the confessions I'd imagined about his parents, this wasn't what I expected.

I nodded. "Okay."

"As the years progressed and they had two sons, they became more paranoid. Or that's how my brother and I saw it. We didn't realize that they were just scared for their family, for our safety." His gaze hardened as he looked away. "And the government basically dismissed their worries and gave them no help. Absolutely zero help."

"So, was there someone after them?"

Zack's gaze flew to mine, and his handsome features turned stern. "Absolutely. And they did everything they could to protect us. They paid the ultimate sacrifice."

I gasped in horror. "Zack, I didn't know…"

He shook his head. "How could you? I always acted like their deaths were a freak accident."

"I just… I'm at a loss for words."

"A terror organization thought my parents had more clout than they did, and so they became targets right before my parents moved back here. There was a bounty on my parents." He shook his head. "They didn't have a chance, but they did their best. They got us to age before it happened."

My heart burned in sorrow for Zack and Ian.

That kind of loss.

That kind of terror.

"You always grew up feeling like you had to look over your shoulder?" I asked softly, taking a step closer to Zack.

He nodded. "Always, but they never told us why until we were older. But they'd taught us martial arts, survival skills, urban combat skills." He sighed. "While other kids were learning to ride bikes, we were learning hand-to-hand combat. My brother and I tried to rebel, and we thought they were crazy... like some of those survivalists who go off the grid. Up until I was ten or eleven, I just wanted to grow up in a normal house. I didn't understand why I had to have the crazy parents. I just wished they'd told us sooner."

The pain radiated to me, and I couldn't stand still. I looped my arms around Zack, wishing I could share in the pain he felt, take it away...

I rested my head on his chest, listening to the steady rhythm of his heart.

"So we both know what it feels like to carry the world's weight on our shoulders," I said softly, tilting my head to look into his striking hazel eyes. "Why didn't you tell me sooner?"

"I didn't want to scare you. I didn't want you to think the entire world was full of bad stuff." His voice was tender and his gaze even more so.

"I had you. You're the good stuff, Zack."

"Then why not good enough to stay, Sadie?"

His words were like a million nails to the heart, and I had no answer.

I didn't know why I wanted to run.

But even now, every cell in my body felt ready to explode, ready to dart at the first hint of disaster.

And now, with Tim running around, I felt like all I could do was go away where no one could find me.

That would be my peace.

Isolation.

"It wasn't you, Zack. It's me. I don't have my head screwed on straight." I took a step back. "Even now, all I can think about is how good it feels to be in your arms, to be with you. You're my safety net, but you shouldn't have to be. That was never anything I looked for before in a partner. So, why now? Why base my entire future on something that happened to me in the past?"

His eyes stormed with emotion as he nodded slowly. "We understand each other so well, Sadie, because we've both faced demons we didn't ever want to believe existed. But this world isn't always rainbows and butterflies."

"I know, Zack." I nodded, feeling a shiver through me. "But I understand what my therapist means about falling in love with someone who shared that trauma with me."

Zack bit his lip and shook his head. "That's the thing, Sadie. It wasn't traumatic for me. That's what I do. I rescue people. I protect people. It was traumatic for you, and whether it was me who saved you or my brother or one of Jaxson's brothers, you'd still have all those memories leading up to the rescue. Those can't be taken away. Reminders will exist in this world of the horrors you faced." He leaned against an enormous Douglas fir trunk and crossed his arms. "I get that I remind you of that moment in your life. I can accept that you don't want to be reminded of that moment. But I want to believe that maybe that moment you saw me, and I held you as I carried you out of the warehouse, was the beginning of good things to come. That's how I wish your therapist wanted to frame what happened to you because I'm telling you, Sadie…" He scratched his chin and let out a deep breath. "You'll be running for a long time trying to grasp a peace that might not exist."

Honesty dripped from his words.

"I know…"

Zack's eyes narrowed on me, and a wave of longing swept over me. "Do you, though? Because I will not be the only reminder you'll face throughout the coming years. Triggers will sneak up on you when you least expect it, and if it were me, I'd rather have someone I trusted right there with me to guide me through them."

Every word he said was the truth.

My therapist was wrong.

I needed Zack.

But the damage was done.

I'd let him go.

He propped himself off the tree and cleared his throat. "If we used your therapist's analogy, I should ditch my brother because the worst thing in our world happened in front of us. I'm sure whenever he looks at me, he thinks of that day our parents were taken away because I know when I look at him, I think the same." He ran his fingers through his hair. "But do you know what that shared experience brings, Sadie?"

I shook my head, feeling my throat constrict from his honesty.

"Comfort." He took a few steps forward. "And the fact that I couldn't bring that to you shows my failures as a partner to you, Sadie. And I'm sorry. I'll regret that for the rest of my life."

Tears pricked my eyes as I blinked away the dampness. "It's not like that, Zack." I brought in a trembling breath. "You were the bright spot in all of it. I don't think I could have gotten through the night terrors without you. I just…" I shook my head. "I just need time and space."

He nodded, wrapping his arm around my shoulders and squeezing me close. "I get it, but I'll always be here for you. Now, let's get you to that appointment."

I chuckled, shaking my head. "Do we have to?"

I wasn't sure, but it felt like Zack pressed a soft kiss on top of my knit cap before we started toward the house.

On the third step, he stopped walking and turned

around. I nearly bumped into him. His fiery gaze landed on mine as he cupped his hands around my face.

"I can't keep pretending, Sadie."

My heart battered inside my chest as I silently begged for a kiss. Zack's lips met mine, and I opened my mouth as our kisses went from controlled to ragged and torn with uncertainty. His lips tasted like peppermint as he slid his tongue to dance with mine. A fiery need crept through me as I let out a soft moan of appreciation. Our kisses warmed me from the chill in the air as he pulled me closer, pressing his firm body against mine.

My phone alarm chimed, and I groaned as his mouth broke from mine.

"It's the reminder for my session."

Zack smiled, his eyes connecting with mine.

The thought of having to talk to my therapist pained me. I felt like I got more out of the last twenty minutes with Zack than I had these last several months with her. But that was just it. I didn't need my boyfriend to be my therapist. It wasn't fair to him.

But, man, it felt good being in his arms…

The way he squeezed me close as we hiked back

to his house made me forget the morning and gave me a promise of peace, even if it wasn't long-lived.

We reached the front door, and he punched in his code and opened the door, letting me out of his arms.

A shiver ran through me as the warmth of the house reminded me of just how cold I was.

Zack helped me out of my coat, and I caught Ian watching us, which made him smile.

"Don't mind me. I'm just over here working." Ian grinned.

I forced a chuckle and glanced at Zack. "Thank you for sharing that with me about your parents."

His eyes held mine, and he softly touched my chin. "I should have done it sooner."

"The timing was perfect. It was what I needed to hear. I'm just sorry it ever happened."

Zack and his brother traded a glance, and I swallowed down the swelling of emotions threatening to crumple me into a ball.

"I'd better get going to my appointment." Without thinking, I stood on my toes and swiped a quick kiss against Zack's cheek, and his breath caught.

I tightened my fists as I turned around and started toward the stairs to my bedroom. I shouldn't toy with him like that. I didn't expect to kiss him, but it just felt so natural.

With each step up, I became surer of my decision.

I was going to end my sessions with my therapist. She laid the framework, but now it was up to me to make the decisions that would let me live life again.

Chapter Fourteen

Zack

"So, you told her about our parents?" Ian's gaze locked on mine.

"Vaguely," I responded, feeling the tautness of my spine. The moment I told her, every muscle in my body had contracted, and I felt sick.

I didn't need to be reprimanded by my brother now, too.

"Why would you do that?"

My eyes snapped to his. "Because I love her, Ian. I lost her because I wasn't honest with her, because I didn't change any part of my life to be with her. It's too late to win her back, but the least I can do is let her know she's not alone in this world. That maybe, just maybe, there are other ways to deal with evil things in this world." I shook my head and took a seat. "Does that make any sense to you?"

"Yeah, more than you know."

"Then there you go."

My brother walked over and shut the door to my office before sitting across from me.

He stared vacantly at the floor. "I don't think Sadie's telling you everything."

I straightened in the chair, folding my hands behind my head as I kicked my legs out in front of me, watching my brother.

"What are you talking about?"

"I don't believe this is the first time she's heard from her ex."

"Okay…"

Ian brought his gaze to meet mine. "I guess what I'm saying is that I'd be careful what all you tell her about our parents."

Anger rose through me. I knew and trusted Sadie more than anyone. I also knew she was in pain, and that agony was pushing her to make decisions she might later regret.

But not to trust her?

"For what reason?"

"Like I said, I don't think she's being truthful about Tim." Ian's face crumpled. "And I don't know that we need her to know everything about our past."

"Ian, before all this went down, you knew I was going to ask her to marry me. To join us in our business. And now you're telling me you suddenly don't trust her?"

Ian's expression softened as he stood, pacing. "I don't mean for it to sound like that. It's just things aren't adding up. Like, why would someone put those things in her apartment?"

"What? You think she did it herself?" I was stunned my brother would even think it. We'd spent our lives helping victims, and now he was turning on one?

"I was talking to Melanie, and she'd mentioned that Sadie hadn't been acting herself lately."

I scrunched my face in disbelief. "Of course, she hasn't been feeling herself lately. Someone's been watching her."

"Allegedly."

I stood, raking my fingers through my hair in frustration. "Wow. I can't believe you're saying this stuff, Ian."

"I'm the one who can look at things objectively."

"Since when have you started chatting with Melanie?" I asked, standing in front of my brother.

Ian flinched as if I'd slapped him, and maybe I should have. Why would he ever accuse Sadie of something like this? He was with me when we rescued her. He knows firsthand what she'd been put through.

Tension tore through the room as I stared down my brother. "What are you really trying to say?"

"I'm not trying to say anything, accuse anyone, or... Listen, some of the dots aren't connecting. That's all."

I shook my head. "That's not how I see it at all. Why don't you provide me with some proof?"

"It's not like there's proof of any of this. That's

not what I'm saying. I have a hunch that she's been in contact with Tim off and on through the years. Melanie had mentioned that a guy had called for her a couple of times."

"Had Sadie picked up?"

Ian nodded.

My stomach felt suddenly sour. "While we were together?"

He slid his hands together. "Yeah."

"Any other so-called evidence?"

"I saw a couple of messages going to someone who no longer has an active profile. They only had initials remaining."

"And?"

"The initials were T.V.."

I drew a breath. "When?"

"A few years ago."

Relief briefly spread through me. "Listen, I appreciate what you're doing, but Sadie is the victim in all of this. She didn't reach out to her psycho ex."

My brother didn't look convinced. "I'm meeting Melanie for dinner tonight. I'll find out more."

I clenched my jaw together and glanced out the window to see a few sparse snowflakes floating through the frigid air.

"Fine. Keep me posted."

"Nothing has ever come between us," Ian said, taking a step closer. "I'm not trying to accuse Sadie of anything. It's just she's been through a lot, and maybe on some level she craved…"

That was the exact opposite of what she craved.

"I think you've said enough."

Ian nodded and let himself out of my office.

Sadie was more intelligent than most. She certainly wouldn't be dumb enough to hand over her phone or laptop if there were something incriminating on it.

Just the thought made my blood boil.

And what was going on with Melanie? Why was she suddenly turning on her friend?

Was she that upset about her coffee shop? It wasn't Sadie's fault.

I sat down and hung my head in my hands, groaning away the headache that was attempting to roar to life.

The mere mention of my parents had brought back a flood of emotions with a suffocating intensity that made years of grief suddenly feel insignificant.

But telling Sadie what little I had somehow made me feel slightly lighter.

Even though it hurt like hell now.

I shook my head with a growl and stood. It wasn't like I could bring my parents back, but I could make them proud from where they were now. I'd always hoped they'd look down on Ian and me and realize everything they'd taught us had helped a large group of people.

There'd always been so much I'd wanted to tell my parents and couldn't, like how sorry I was for doubting their intentions.

My stomach squeezed at the thought, and I let out another deep breath.

Things would be okay. I'd help Sadie through this, and we'd go our separate ways.

It was better that way.

I shook my head as if that would convince me of it more and walked out of the office.

Sadie was bounding down the stairs with her laptop folded in her hands.

"How'd it go?" I asked before looking at her expression.

Her eyes met mine but were red-rimmed from tears. "Not that great."

I chuckled. "Yeah, I see that now."

She handed me her laptop. "Your brother mentioned that you wanted to see this."

"Oh, thanks." I took the device from her as she turned down the hall to where I heard her sister and Jaxson talking. "Hey, Sadie?"

She turned around. "Yeah?"

"Did Tim ever call you at the coffee shop?"

Her brows furrowed in confusion, and she shook her head. "Not that I'm aware of. I mean, I didn't speak to him."

"Cool."

Sadie's head tilted. "Why?"

"I just want to have my ducks in a row when I talk to Officer Carl later."

She smiled and nodded. "Thanks, Zack. I

appreciate it, and I'm sorry for all this trouble my life has caused you."

"Don't say that, Sadie. You're my…" I stopped myself. "No problem."

"Oh, and I stopped my therapy sessions as of today." A twinkle bounded through her gaze.

I couldn't hide my surprise. "Well, congratulations."

She laughed. "Well, I realized that just talking with you outside earlier made me feel better than months of droning on with her."

I nodded, smiling and trying to tamp down the spark of hope that erupted. "You have my number."

Sadie chuckled, turning back around as she went down the hall to her sister. "Oh, and my password is capital Z, small a, c, and k, along with the number 4, and then the word ever."

I couldn't hide my smile as I nodded, returning to my office and setting the laptop on my desk.

Typing in her password, I felt a bubbling pressure build in my chest. I didn't want to find anything that even hinted at my brother being right.

Sadie wasn't like that.

The idea of someone trying to hurt Sadie didn't do wonders for my own well-being, but I wanted to believe that I was objective enough to still watch out for cues that could lead us in a surprising direction. I didn't believe that the direction Melanie and my brother suddenly started down had anything to do with Sadie or her ex.

I puckered my mouth and blew out air as I clicked on the first social media app she used, scrolling through the messages.

I landed on the old message from someone with the initials T.V., no profile picture, and the last message sent years ago. My teeth sank into my lip as I clicked on the message chain and noticed a few innocuous messages going back and forth, reminiscing, but nothing romantic. It wasn't until I landed on one that caught my eye, asking about dating his brother.

I narrowed my eyes to her response, which was a simple *no*.

And T.V. never asked again.

Tapping my fingers, I wondered who this person

was and why Sadie hadn't mentioned anything about them.

Probably because it was irrelevant.

I looked through her other apps, hoping for some clue to bring us directly to Tim Venson's intentions or any missteps.

My phone rang, and I glanced down to see Officer Carl's number pop up on the screen.

"Hey, there, Zack. How's it going?"

"Pretty good. I'm just staying warm with the first season's flakes coming down. You?"

"Ah, I'm in my cruiser, freezing to death, but I'm hanging in there. I wanted to let you know that I did a little poking around in town, and I had several sightings of that fellow you sent over."

My heart hammered in my chest.

So, Tim was here.

"Yeah? Where's he been spotted?"

"Surprisingly, or maybe not so surprisingly..." Officer Carl chuckled like he was a kid caught with his hand in the cookie jar. "Joe over at the hardware store recognized him immediately, and so did Carol over at the all-night diner. Apparently, Tim loves coconut cream pie."

"Could you get a feel for how long he's been around?"

"It sounds like a week or so, but they haven't seen him for a day or so."

My knee bobbed up and down with nervous energy. The asshole was here.

"This is very helpful, Officer. Thanks for sniffing around for us."

"Absolutely. Just don't do anything I wouldn't."

I laughed, squeezing my fists together. "I'm not sure that limits the scope all that much."

Office Carl laughed. "Possibly. I've also had some interesting developments on that break-in, but I'll let you know more when I have a clearer direction."

"Thanks. Appreciate it." I was ready to hang up and talk to Sadie, but the officer wasn't finished.

"Hey, I know it's not my place, but I thought I saw your brother with Melanie earlier. Are they an item?"

"It would be news to me." But it would explain

some things.

"Then you didn't hear the news from me, but a deputy spotted them making out in a parked car over by the resort."

I shivered, trying to push the thought out of my head. "Good to know my brother hasn't written off women then, Officer. Thanks for the heads-up."

"My pleasure."

And this time, he finally hung up.

I made my way to the kitchen where Jaxson, Elena, and Sadie huddled around the island.

"I got some interesting news from Officer Carl," I announced, sliding the laptop to Sadie.

She wouldn't meet my gaze, which concerned me, but one problem at a time.

"Tim has been spotted around town for the last week or so."

Horror flashed across Sadie's features. "I was hoping it was all a coincidence."

"That would be one hell of a coincidence." Jaxson's strained laughter cut the tension.

"But I have some questions for you, Sadie. I'm

confused by what I saw in your messages."

Sadie lifted her gaze to mine, and curiosity flared through her brilliant green eyes. "Oh, really? Sure. Ask away."

Chapter Fifteen

Sadie

"Who is T.V.?" Zack asked.

I shook my head, frowning. "I don't know. I'm guessing Tim Venson. Why?"

"Because there's some old messages with an obsolete profile with the initials T.V."

"From when?" I opened the lid of my laptop.

"It's been years," Zack offered. "And it was something about a brother."

Shock registered through me. How could I forget about her?

"Oh, my gosh. That was Tim's sister." I let out a groan. "I can't believe how good I did at blocking all of that out."

Elena lifted her right brow. "You were messaging with Tracy?"

"Stupidly, yes. But we were friends, and then when everything happened, I didn't know how to get her to kind of... go away." I sighed, rubbing my temples. "But when she started to bring up dating her brother again, I just dropped her. The crazy thing is that I only met her once when I first started dating Tim, but we clicked and just spent time messaging. I think she was seventeen or so when I was nineteen. Anyway, I didn't want to penalize her just because her brother is nuts."

Zack let out a deep breath. "That makes sense."

Elena laughed, glancing at Zack. "Hardly. Our Dad would have killed you if he knew you were still talking with anyone from that family."

"It's been years." I shook my head, feeling a shiver. "I just totally forgot about her, but I haven't heard from any of them until that first message."

"Well, knowing that Tim has been wandering

around Granite Peak tells us we need to stay alert."

Jaxson nodded, and I realized the buzz from Zack kissing the top of my head earlier was quickly disappearing. "Absolutely."

"Well, the good news is that none of us has to cook. I ordered pizza. It should be delivered any second," my sister chimed in.

"You and food." I laughed, realizing I hadn't eaten anything today.

My nerves were shot, and it didn't help that when I texted Melanie earlier, she didn't respond. Speaking of, I picked up my phone and messaged her a friendly message to check on her.

"Everything okay?" Zack asked.

I nodded, leaning on the counter. "Yeah. Melanie's not responding to my messages, but other than that, I'm fine."

Zack looked perplexed, and then a frown moved across his handsome features. "Well, I think she and my brother have been hanging out a bit."

My brows rose in surprise. "Really?"

"Yeah, that's what I managed to gather from my

189

brother and a few eyes around town."

"That's new."

Zack nodded. "I'd say so."

He looked like he wanted to say something else, but something on my phone caught his attention. "Looks like you might have received a reply."

My eyes dropped to the screen, and I saw Melanie's reply.

Hey, girl. Totally fine. Hope you're too. I'm going out on a date soon. I think it's probably better if you take a few days off until everything gets sorted. Ian told me a little bit more about what's going on.

"Well, so much for going into Granite Beans tomorrow." I sighed, pushing my phone to Zack. "And it sounds like you're right on about Melanie and your brother."

Zack leaned over and glanced at my phone. He rested his hand on my shoulder, which sent a charge through me.

The gate buzzed, and I glanced at my phone to

see the pizza delivery. I unlocked it, and he drove through.

"Umm, Sadie. Didn't Melanie say to you that she had sent you messages, but you didn't respond, so that's why she came to the house to check on you?"

I nodded. "Yeah, and I never got them. I didn't get them until the next morning, actually."

"That's because that's when she sent them."

The doorbell rang, and Jaxson glanced at me. "Pizza. I'll go grab it."

The air turned tight around us with the same apprehension that filled me when I first saw her messages suddenly appear. I knew deep down that these had been fresh texts, but then the message from Tim just pushed everything aside.

"You don't think they just got caught up in the cell service abyss?" I asked, already knowing the answer.

"I don't." He let out a deep breath as Elena glanced at me.

"And how long have you known her?" my sister asked.

"Since I've moved here, basically."

Zack nodded. "She bought out the previous owners of the coffee shop right before Sadie moved here, if my memory serves me right."

"She's been nothing but sweet and supportive of me, so I don't know what she'd have to gain by pretending she texted or stopped by," I explained, ignoring the pit in my stomach. "It's probably just some weird coincidence."

Jaxson brought in two colossal pizza boxes. "Very rarely are there coincidences," he said, setting the pizza on the counter.

I laughed and nodded. "I'll try to get better at remembering that."

The rest of the evening went by in a blur of near normalcy. It felt so good to be sharing pizza and beer with my sister and her husband and to have Zack by my side.

We didn't talk about Carmella or Tim. We just focused on the present.

But the moment I sensed it winding down and Elena and Jaxson wandered off to bed, I felt like I was suddenly suffocating. A jittery nervousness ran through my shoulders as I glanced at Zack. The idea of being in bed alone tonight made me apprehensive.

I pushed the last few slices of pizza into a plastic baggie and noticed my hands trembling as I put the pizza in the fridge.

Everything was going to be okay.

I was fine.

Tim won't get me here.

But the tension building between my shoulder blades roared to life when I turned around and didn't see Zack.

The silence of the night stretched to deafening heights as I closed my eyes and focused on being okay. I was surrounded by family and a man who still loved me.

"Zack?" I said softly, trying to clear my throat.

A few of the lights had been turned off, and I thought it was strange he hadn't said goodnight.

"You're being ridiculous, Sadie," I hummed to myself as I washed my hands. "Everything's fine. You'll be fine."

"Hey, there." Zack's gruff voice wrapped around

me like a comforting embrace, and the tension nearly vanished. "You okay?"

I turned around slowly, drying off my hands, and smiled. "Actually, no. I wouldn't say I'm doing great. It feels like every nerve in my body is on high alert. I can't even get my shoulders to relax. My mind can't stop racing. I'm even conjuring up crazy thoughts about Melanie and her involvement in some abstract way. So, no... I think I have to admit I'm not okay."

Tenderness weaved through Zack's expression as he raised both hands and slowly ran them over my arms. "It's okay to not be okay."

"You always know the right things to say, Zack."

He winked at me, and the familiar flutter of anticipation flew through me. "Not always, or you'd still be mine."

"I really appreciate everything you and your brother have done for me. I didn't mean to add this complication. I thought Carmella was enough."

"She's more than enough," Zack agreed, slowly sliding his hands along my arms to my back. "But you have nothing to apologize for."

He took a step forward, closing the space between us. My body hummed with the pull to Zack I always felt as I looked into his eyes.

"I still love you, Zack." My confession took me by surprise.

A flitter of heat ran through his gaze. "I've never stopped loving you, but I'm sure you know that."

My heart hammered in my chest as his lips hovered near mine. "I'm just so sorry I can't move on from my past. I'm sorry I've hurt you and made promises I can't keep."

"I told you that you never have to apologize to me, and I mean it." Zack shook his head. "You've never made me a promise you couldn't keep, Sadie. I'm the one who couldn't keep my promises. I wasn't there for you enough."

I shook my head, hating that he carried guilt for how things had worked out between us. "You were always open with me. I knew from the beginning that your job took you away for long stretches. I didn't expect my mind to betray me. I thought I was strong enough to be... alone."

And that alone scared me for my future. Carmella would get out of jail.

Which was why I had my plan.

To land in a place where no one could ever find me.

The idea pressed heavily on me as I looked into Zack's beautiful eyes.

"Let's just get through this without any promises but with hope." His voice lowered. "And don't forget about your dreams, Sadie. Even if I'm not your partner, I'd love to help you fulfill them."

His words sank deep into my soul, and the heat of need pummeled through me as I leaned against him, feeling the strength behind the man.

"Thank you, Zack," I whispered, running my hands along his arms.

His mammoth size towered over me and made me feel protected, and most of all, heard.

Zack's eyes dropped to my lips, and I felt warmth pool in my belly, sinking deeper with every passing second.

Right when I was going to ask him to kiss me, his

mouth came down to mine, and he pulled my body into his as tightly as possible.

He let out a low growl of need as my lips parted, and I felt his tongue slide against mine. The way his hand curled through my hair while his other softly slid along my neck made me wish for so much more.

"Sadie, you taste even better than I remember," he whispered between kisses.

His mouth stayed over mine, and I couldn't push away how right things felt in his arms. It was like nothing else mattered, as if the world were right again.

I tugged on his shirt, and he smiled against my mouth as my hand skittered underneath the fabric. His chiseled physique felt warm but solid like he always had.

Without thinking, I pulled away and broke our kiss as his eyes fluttered open.

"Sadie, I'm sorry."

I shook my head, smiling slowly. "Take me to bed."

His eyes turned fierce with need as his lips curled into the most gorgeous smile. "Absolutely."

Zack pulled me close, kissing me with a renewed

sense of desire as I moved my hands up to his face, cupping his cheeks as our kisses turned more frantic. Looping my arms around his neck, I gave a little hop, and he caught me as I wrapped my legs around his waist, our mouths still searching for something we both craved.

The firm grip of his hands under my butt as he carried me down the hall made my stomach burn with anticipation.

When we reached a guest room on the main floor, he slowly kicked it open and shut it just as easily in the darkness.

Breaking his mouth from mine, his breaths were ragged with the same need I felt. "Sadie, are you sure?"

Seeing the shadow of his smile and only a glint in his eyes from the faint glow of the outside porch light, I nodded. "Absolutely."

"Sadie, I love you so much." His voice was low and rough with need as he pushed my back against the wall, my legs still wrapped around him. My head lolled to the side as his mouth slid along the bare skin of my neck, nibbling and licking with each passing beat of my heart.

The need for Zack was intense and burning as his hardness rubbed against the fabric of my pants. I let out a little murmur as I tried to whisper his name, but it just turned into a moan as his tongue traced along my collarbone before he lifted my sweater over my head, tossing it to the floor.

My body felt weak from desire as he unfastened the front clasp of my bra, exposing my breasts. I could see his smile widen as he cupped one in his hand and slowly sucked on the other. Tingles pricked through my entire body as I squeezed my legs harder around his waist.

With each tug and lick of Zack's tongue, my body nearly ached as I let out a little whimper. He stopped, bringing his mouth to mine before spinning me around in his arms and moving us to the bed.

He quickly pulled off his shirt as I scooted my pants and underwear down my legs, kicking them to the edge of the bed.

"I missed your curves," he said gruffly as my fingers slid along his waistband, helping him to unbutton his pants.

"I missed everything about you," I whispered.

He unzipped his pants and pushed them down. Even in the shadows of the bedroom, I could see his length as he propped himself up on his elbows.

Zack moved his fingers slowly along my belly, resting them in between my legs, which entirely undid me as he kissed me, nudging me wider with his knee.

I couldn't help but kiss Zack harder and deeper, feeling completely unrestrained as his fingers slid along my lips.

Everything about Zack was perfection. He knew my body and mind better than I did. I slid my arms around his neck as his kisses slowed, and he brought his lips back to my breasts. I nestled my head into the crook of his neck and inhaled everything about him as his fingers teased me to the edge.

"Zack," I panted, feeling his fingers slow. "I need you. All of you."

He rumbled a little laugh of need as he took away his hand and ran his thick fingers along my ribcage, sending a flutter of goosebumps along my skin. He brushed his thumbs along my nipples as he slid into me, stretching me to my limits and letting me fill with desire. His mouth replaced his thumb on my nipple as he sucked and teased me with ease.

I gasped in ecstasy as he moved slowly inside, bringing his mouth back down to mine. His tongue danced with mine as he moved his hips in a rhythm meant only for us.

The fullness inside me as my world felt safe and the secrets forgotten made me wish for a different ending. I wanted Zack, and I was tired of fighting my demons.

As he thrust once more, ecstasy rushed through every single cell in my body. My moans collided with his as if I had no control over anything rational any longer. I felt his release as my world spun into a frantic collision with reality, my legs squeezing around him as he opened his eyes to look at me.

"Sadie, I love you. We need to make this work."

Even with the darkness in the room, the glassiness of his eyes couldn't be missed.

I nodded, knowing I was lying to the one man who could give me my dream.

And I couldn't do it.

I slowly slid out from under him, kissing him as I did so, and grabbed my clothes.

Zack had been the only man who knew how to take me over that edge, and I knew that I could be free with him and let my emotions and sounds run wild with him.

No judgment ever.

But I also knew that he deserved someone who wasn't going to be looking over her shoulder all the time, and once Carmella was rereleased, the cycle would start over.

Not to mention Tim.

He couldn't babysit me for the rest of our lives, and I certainly wouldn't want that.

"I don't want my sister to get any ideas," I explained, pulling on my clothes.

He sat up and nodded with a sexy smirk. "And what ideas are those?"

I didn't say anything as I tugged my sweater over my head. "You know, sisterly gossip."

Zack nodded, pulling on his pants, and let out a

deep sigh. "You felt so good, Sadie. It's like you belong in my arms."

I couldn't disagree. It did feel right.

He stood and pulled me close. Feeling the strength in his arms brought instant comfort.

My lips still felt swollen, and I didn't want the feeling to go away. It was such a beautiful reminder of what I had with the man I loved.

"When I'm with you, it's like the fear just vanishes," I said softly.

He touched the tip of my nose and kissed it. "Then maybe that means we're meant to do more of this."

I smiled. "It just might, but not…"

Zack nodded, interrupting the words I didn't even want to say, and brushed a piece of hair from my cheek. "Ready for bed?"

"Beyond." I smiled as we left the guest room and quietly made our way upstairs.

I stopped in front of the guest room I'd been staying in, and his lips turned down when he realized where I planned on sleeping.

"Sorry… I just—"

He kissed me, interrupting my apology, and stepped away. "See you in the morning, Sadie."

I nodded, feeling numb as I walked into the bedroom and quickly tugged off my clothes. Reaching for my suitcase, I pulled out a pair of pajamas and let out a sigh, wishing I could memorize every second of sleeping with Zack.

As I pulled on my jammies, my gaze landed on the windowsill, and the entire room turned icy.

There was a small seashell propped on the sill.

Tim had been in my room.

Chapter Sixteen

Zack

The last three days felt like an eternity. Sadie had grown distant, and I understood why.

I had failed her.

I'd promised her she would be safe at my house and that no one could get to her, and somehow, Tim had.

Ian, Jaxson, and I had scoured the security footage and found absolutely nothing. There wasn't a shadow, a bunny, or even a branch falling to trip the security cameras, and that especially included no Tim.

The cameras picked up Sadie and me roaming the woods, kissing, and walking back to the house. It showed Jaxson and Elena taking walks in the evenings. It showed Ian coming up to the house. It captured the pizza driver that night. Sadie found the trinket but no Tim.

"We'll find him," Ian assured me. "We were taught that every security system has a hole. It's our job to figure out where that void is and fill it."

I stared at my brother and nodded. "I know. The problem is that we haven't filled it. There've been no sightings around town, either."

"Maybe he went back," my brother offered.

"I'm starting to think that could be the case." I ran my palms over my face and groaned. "I'd imagine he has to show up for his job. The last one listed was as a software analyst, and when I called the firm, they verified his employment as of three days ago."

"Ah, the joys of remote work, a stalker's delight." Ian nodded and pushed himself off the couch. "I'm meeting Melanie for dinner. Is there anything else I can do? I fly out tomorrow to New Mexico for that job we took on. I have a team meeting me there in the afternoon."

"No. I'm fine. Thanks for picking up the slack."

He smiled and shook his head. "It's what we do."

"So are you and Melanie…?"

Ian's mouth pulled into a smile. "Yeah. Things are going well so far."

I was truly happy for my brother. I just hoped that Melanie wasn't skewing his views on Sadie, and I couldn't even fathom why they could be a thing.

I laughed. "Don't do anything I wouldn't do."

"That doesn't set the bar real high, does it?" Ian did a quick wave as Sadie came bounding down the hall, nearly colliding with him.

"Now that's what I love to see," I said, smiling at her.

"Guess what?" Her eyes sparkled in a way I hadn't seen in a long time.

"What?"

I think I already knew.

"Carmella is officially booked. Her prison ID is 1707A1, and I don't have to think about her for at least a few years." Her grin was wider than I'd seen for weeks, and it made me wish I could produce the same response in her, but none of that mattered.

All that mattered was that Sadie felt better. She could finally breathe in a deep breath without worrying about Carmella around the corner. We just needed to ensure the same about Tim.

Ian gave Sadie a quick hug. "Congrats. We'll get this other bastard, and you can start living your life again."

Her cheeks blushed, and she glanced at me. "Thanks."

Ian nodded and walked out the front door as Sadie dove into my arms for a hug.

The warmth filled my soul as I felt her body relax into mine.

"I can't believe she's finally gone, at least for a few years." She looked up into my eyes. "I'll just take what peace I can get."

I nodded. "It's all we can do."

She took a step back. "I know this might sound crazy, but can we go celebrate?"

My chest tightened. "You mean out?"

Sadie giggled, and she knew that was my weakness. I loved her giggles and laughs. It was like a melody that wrapped around me and dropped me to my knees.

"Yeah. You know what? I was talking to my brother about Tim, and I don't even think he's in town."

Her expression lit up even more. "You don't?"

I shook my head. "I don't, but I think we should still take precautions."

She clasped her hands and squealed, and I knew I'd made the right choice.

"I'll call the resort and get some reservations at the steakhouse. Sound good?" I asked. "Should I make the reservations for four people?"

Sadie smiled and slowly licked her bottom lip, which nearly undid me. "I was thinking just the two of us."

I nodded, smiling. "I would love that."

"Who knows? Maybe there'll be a repeat of the other night?"

I laughed, shaking my head as Sadie wandered down the hall.

It was moments like these when I was reminded of the easiness with Sadie. It was something I'd cherished every time I came back from a job. I knew I could count on the ease of our relationship to make me forget about whatever our clients' crazy demands were or which case was coming up next.

She always made it better, and it killed me that I didn't do the same for her. I missed the cues.

Which was one of the reasons I'd been talking to my brother about stepping back more and opening up a tactical camp here at the house. We were expanding in leaps and bounds, had teams to take on most of our jobs, and it made sense to me to start up a facility that would allow clients to learn self-defense and survivalist skills. Arm them with knowledge.

I never got to share the news with Sadie before she broke up with me, and I knew if I told her when she'd decided to break up with me, she'd think it was some last-ditch effort to appease her, which wasn't the case. So, I kept it to myself.

But maybe tonight, I could tell Sadie, let her know that if what she needed from me was to be home more, I could provide that. I could do anything she needed.

I also knew I needed to take care of this Tim situation. It wasn't as simple as getting a restraining order. Those rarely worked anyway, and we didn't have enough proof to obtain one at this point, anyway.

Quickly calling the resort, I made reservations for an hour from now and asked for a corner booth.

Making my way into the family room, I saw Jaxson on the phone and Sadie and Elena happily talking on the couch.

"I heard you're taking my sister out tonight to celebrate." Elena grinned at me.

"Can't wait," I said, nodding. "She deserves this and more."

Jaxson hung up and walked over to us. "My brother Blake said he saw Tim back at his apartment. As of two hours ago, he's no longer in Granite Peak."

It looked like Sadie was about to fall over with the news.

Elena gasped and hugged her sister with joy.

Sadie's beautiful green eyes connected with

mine, and I could see relief flooding through her gaze.

We didn't know how long this would last, but at least he wasn't here now.

"My brothers are going to keep an eye on him." Jaxson kept his gaze on mine. I knew what he was silently communicating. I knew it, and I appreciated it. But we'd always done things the right way. The clean way.

I wanted to sleep with a clear conscience.

"I think this officially means I'm having way too much wine tonight because I don't have to keep my wits about me." Sadie threw her head back with carefree laughter, and my chest tightened. This was how Sadie deserved to feel every second of every day.

And until I made sure that was possible, I would feel like I'd failed her.

Sadie bounded up from the couch and stretched her arms to the ceiling. "I'm going to put on my nicest outfit that I didn't already ship back home. I definitely can't wait to celebrate. When are the reservations for?"

"We'll leave in like thirty minutes," I told her.

She smiled in my direction and nodded.

"Perfect."

Elena followed her out of the room, and Jaxson cleared his throat.

"You doing okay?" Jaxson asked.

"Yeah, of course." I nodded. "It's just nice to see Sadie finally be able to let out a deep breath and not feel like she's looking over her shoulder."

He nodded. "That's no way to live."

I took a seat on the couch. "Yeah."

"What do you have planned next?" he asked, taking in a deep breath.

"In terms of…?"

"Timothy," he said flatly.

"I know it's only a matter of time before he comes back." I stretched my feet out in front of me. "And I think a message needs to be sent."

Jaxson's eyes stayed on mine. "Her father sent one to him years ago."

"And it worked for over a decade."

"Or Tim was just laying in wait, sulking, obsessing, planning…"

These were all things I knew. "Yeah. I get it."

"There are ways of getting information that are faster."

"I know." I brought in my legs and propped my elbows on my knees. The fury I felt pulsing through me was hard to control.

What I really wanted was to find Tim and take care of him myself. I hadn't felt that kind of rage since my parents were taken from me, but all I had to do was look at Sadie. She was worth it.

"He hasn't done anything against the law that could be proven in a court of law. He's sent some messages that were just vague enough to escape legal action. He's allowed to travel to towns where his exes might live. We can't prove he trespassed and left something in Sadie's apartment or my home." I shook my head. "Which leaves very few options to deal with him."

"It does."

Jaxson drew a breath. "You know, we often get a bad rap."

"Who, in particular?"

A wry smile spread across his lips. "My brothers

and me."

I laughed and shook my head. "I think being attached to one of the largest crime organizations can do that to a person. I'm just saying."

He smiled. "We're just misunderstood."

"I know." I let out a sigh. "There was a time when I didn't think two wrongs made a right, and then my parents were killed."

Jaxson nodded. "The legal system can only do so much. They're heavily burdened. They have to prioritize drugs, robberies, murders, abuse... the list goes on."

"The world isn't getting kinder, is it?" I stared at Jaxson, knowing what he was asking me.

"It's not."

"Zack," Sadie's voice was full of panic. "He's going after my parents. I just..." She gulped a cry as Elena and Sadie rushed into the family room.

Jaxson and I bolted out of our seats as Sadie shoved her phone into my hand.

I just realized tonight after a long stroll that I'm not too far from your parents. I wonder how they're doing, especially your father. He seemed so big and burly so many years ago. Now, he seems a little frailer. A little more vulnerable. Do you agree? You can breathe easy, my little seashell. I'm not in your neck of the woods right now, but I might stop by your parents' for a friendly hello.

Sadie's hands trembled as they rose to her mouth, and Elena walked over to Jaxson, nearly collapsing in his arms.

I pulled Sadie into my arms, and I kissed the top of her head as her weight fell into me. I held her tightly, vowing to take care of her.

I wouldn't let what happened to my parents happen to the woman I loved more than life.

Chapter Seventeen

Sadie

My phone rang, and I didn't recognize the number. I glanced at Elena and Jaxson, who were deep in discussion, and Zack was in his office.

I debated for another half a second and answered.

I'm sure you think because I'm behind bars that you're safe, but I want you to understand that you will always be on my mind and the minds of many who know that you know too much.

The phone clicked, and my throat constricted as Elena caught my eyes.

"Sadie, what's wrong?" Elena rushed over with Jaxson right behind.

"It's Carmella. She just called me from jail."

Jaxson scowled. "What? Did you take the collect call?"

I shook my head. "No, but it was Carmella. Just like the last time she called. It was her."

Jaxson took my phone from me while I stared at the wall, feeling pressure build in my chest. I couldn't keep doing this. I couldn't. One minute, I was feeling like the weight of the world had been lifted, and now I was crippled with fear.

Every single breath hurt.

The room around me spun into a tiny web of emotion. It felt like the air was charged with something to hurt my lungs and my body.

"You're going to be okay, Sadie." Elena's arm wrapped around my shoulders as she led me to the stool. "We're here for you. Zack won't let anything happen to you."

"What about Mom and Dad?"

Elena stood in front of me, holding my arms to get a good look at me. I felt numb, like a zombie. My racing thoughts narrowed. I just wanted to run. I wanted to escape it all.

And then he brought my parents into it.

And then she called...

"I don't understand why this is happening. I don't." I looked into my sister's eyes for any hint of a reason.

"I don't either, Sadie."

Jaxson let out a deep breath. "That call wasn't from prison unless she used someone's contraband phone."

"Why go to that much trouble?" I asked, shaking my head. "None of what she did had to do with me. Sure, I was the victim, but she only targeted me because I was close to you and the Volkovs."

Jaxson nodded. "I agree."

I pulled my hands over my face and groaned. "It just doesn't make sense."

But what did make sense was wanting to run

away from it all and start over.

"What's going on?" Zack walked into the room, seeing my tears.

"Carmella just called." Elena drew a breath. "But Jaxson doesn't think it was a prison call."

Zack's eyes filled with wild rage. "Let me see the phone."

I shook my head mindlessly, wanting this nightmare to go away as Jaxson handed him the phone.

"I'll go reach out to the prosecutor. Jack needs to know what's going on." He eyed me, and I nodded, giving him a grateful smile. "At the very least, it might extend her stay."

"Thank you, Zack."

He walked to his office as Elena rubbed my back. "I know it seems like everything in the world is tipping on its axis, and you've got people trying to intimidate you left and right, but we are here. We won't let anything happen to you."

I brought my gaze to hers. "What about Mom and Dad?"

"My brothers are on it. I can promise you that

nothing will happen to your parents."

I nodded mindlessly, knowing that once we married into the Volkov family, they'd do as much as they could to protect us all on some level.

But what kind of life was it when you had to always live behind a veil of fear and worry?

I closed my eyes and drew in a few deep breaths, remembering some of the breathing practices my therapist would have me do.

For once, I was thankful for knowing these calming exercises.

My mind lulled with each steady breath in and exhalation. The voices around me drifted into an abyss of muffled sounds as I thought about the last six months.

Kidnapped.

Rescued.

Love.

Life.

Fear.

Threats.

Anxiety.

My eyes flashed open as my pulse pounded

between my ears, and Zack walked back into the room, handing me the phone.

He was my center, the one thing that could stop me from running.

"It's impossible that Carmella made that call." Zack sat next to me.

"What do you mean? I heard her voice."

Zack pressed his lips together and nodded. "I don't doubt you heard it, but she's still in processing. She didn't make that call."

It felt like I was losing control of reality. I knew who I heard.

"Now, that doesn't mean that she didn't record it while she was out, and then someone called and played it for you," Zack offered as his eyes met mine. "Or it's not her at all."

"What do you mean?"

"Jack doesn't necessarily see or hear remorse when he's spoken to Carmella, but he knows a woman who doesn't want to be in jail. No good would come from her reaching out to you. She'd only hurt herself."

I shrugged. "Then where does that leave me?"

Zack glanced at his phone and smiled. "Ian's date must have gotten cut short. He's coming through the gate."

"He was going out with Melanie tonight?" I asked.

"I thought those were his plans," Zack said, eyeing the front door. "But it's probably better that he's here."

The mere mention of Melanie sent a mix of emotions through me. We'd been close, or at least as close as I could be with someone, and I thought we had a connection. Then there was the break-in at the coffee shop, and it was like she thought I was the one who broke in.

But she did stop by the house to check on me.

Ugh. It was all so confusing, which was why I probably failed at so many relationships. I just couldn't read them correctly.

Except with Zack. He made things as clear as day.

He picked up my hand and squeezed it. "You might feel overwhelmed, but believe me when I tell you we're getting to the end of all this. I promise."

I smiled and brought in a shaky breath. "I thought we weren't going to make promises we couldn't keep?"

Zack pressed his mouth against my temple, kissing gently along my hairline. "I will keep that promise to you, Sadie. This will all be all over soon."

Ian walked into the room and glanced at his brother before his gaze landed on mine.

"You okay? What happened?"

"Good news that Carmella is officially locked away, followed by a call from her with some vague threats, but not to be outdone by my ex letting me know he'd like to visit my parents. Things have been highly productive while you've been away."

"For like fifteen minutes?" Ian shook his head.

"Why are you back?" Zack asked.

"Melanie canceled. She said she had some family stuff to take care of. I thought I could at least make myself useful."

"Are you still up for dinner out?" Zack eyed me, and I couldn't help but laugh.

"Not even a little bit."

Jaxson cleared his throat and stood. "You deserve some levity, Sadie. Your parents will be protected. I already have people watching the house, and my brothers will be there soon. Enjoy the fact that a very nasty woman is behind bars."

Elena folded her hands in her lap and nodded. "Mom and Dad will be fine."

I glanced at Zack, who kept his face expressionless. He had a habit of doing that when he didn't want to persuade me one way or another, which I usually appreciated.

But tonight, I just wanted to be told.

Zack's lip curled slightly, and he held out his hand. "You look beautiful. Let's go out tonight and enjoy some wine and steak."

I looked into Zack's eyes and saw something that made my heart clench so tightly it almost burst. I saw a love so clear and so pure that my mind felt dizzy. He had the power to break me or let me rise, and he always chose to let me rise.

My hand slipped into his, and he helped me up. Elena clapped and laughed. "It's about time. I'm going to call Mom and Dad to let them know what's been going on and to see how they're doing."

I stopped in my tracks. "Should I stay? I can wait for that. I don't want—"

Elena chuckled. "Go. They've been worried sick about your staying at the house the whole time."

"Okay, fine. Tell them I'll call them after dinner."

"They'll be in bed after you get back." Elena smiled warmly and nodded. "But I'll let them know."

I gave my sister a quick hug and followed Zack down the hallway toward the mudroom. He helped me get my coat on, which didn't match my outfit at all, but it was all I had since I'd shipped everything east.

When he opened the garage, the brisk air woke me up as we made our way to his Jeep.

"We'll take this one tonight. They've been talking about snow flurries all day."

"Always love a fun Jeep ride." I climbed into the front seat and shut the door as Zack did the same. I glanced at him from the corner of my eyes and couldn't help but be struck by how good-looking he was, no matter what the situation called for.

My mind couldn't help but wonder what his parents would be like if they were still here. And what took them away? In between everything going on, I still couldn't help but wonder what actually happened.

Comfortable silence hung between us as we drove along the mountain road toward Granite Peak's resort. I tried so hard to reach for that brief moment of jubilation when I knew Carmella was no longer roaming the streets and Tim wasn't in Washington…

Before it all came crashing down.

Zack slid his hand over to my knee and softly rubbed my leg as we turned into the drive of the resort.

I needed this. He probably did, too.

Driving up to the grand resort brought so many amazing memories back. The nights that Zack would bring me here for a quick lunch or an evening of drinks and dinner. One weekend, he'd even planned a little getaway for us, even though he only lived ten minutes away.

It was all these things that made me fall in love with Zack.

He parked the car and came over to my side, helping me out of the Jeep. A gust of wind blew, and he wrapped his arms around me, bringing me close as we walked up to the lobby. The valet greeted us, opening the doors as we walked into the mammoth lobby with timber pillars, a gigantic cobblestone fireplace roiling in the corner, and a sitting area featuring green velvet Chesterfield couches facing one another with an oversized matching ottoman.

As we walked through the lobby toward the restaurant, he bent down and whispered, "Have I told you how beautiful you are?"

The warmth of his breath left me wanting more from the man I couldn't promise tomorrow to, but I wanted to so badly.

"You're not half bad yourself," I teased.

His hand rested on my waist as the hostess greeted us. Her name was Natalie, and we came to know her pretty well, considering how often we stopped in.

She showed us to the corner table overlooking the ski mountain, but I knew Zack had requested this table because he could also see the entire restaurant.

We slid into the booth, and Zack kept his hand on my knee as the hostess handed us menus and rattled off the drink specials.

When she left, I turned slightly in the booth to get a better look at Zack. He'd somehow managed to change into a crisp white button-down shirt, sleeves rolled up slightly, and a pair of jeans. The strength behind his hazel eyes and the way his jawline strengthened into his chin were nothing less than perfection. And none of that mattered because underneath it all, his heart was pure. His love was pure.

"I know I've said it before, but I can't thank you and your brother enough. You've done so much for me, and you continue to do so much."

His fingers tangled with mine under the table. "Sadie, you have nothing to thank me for. I'm just so glad that, for once, I can do something to help someone I love."

"You've done more than you'll ever know." I nodded, dipping my gaze to the menu.

"What aren't you telling me?" he asked softly. "Ever since I came back to town, I've known there's something you're keeping a secret. If it will help us in any way, please tell me. I won't judge you. Nothing matters to me more than keeping you safe."

My eyes flashed to his, and a wave of guilt flooded through me. I took a few deep breaths just as the server appeared.

We quickly ordered our drinks and dinner. We knew the menu by heart, and I always loved the Steak Diane.

"Please tell me, Sadie."

I closed my eyes briefly and willed myself to be brave enough to tell him.

"I've been contemplating starting over." My eyes connected with his.

He nodded, keeping his hazel eyes locked on mine. "I can understand that."

I bit my lip, feeling a gnawing sensation growing deep in my abdomen. "I mean away from it all."

The server dropped off my martini and a club soda for Zack. I took a sip as he studied me.

"You mean away from everyone?"

"Something like that," I confessed. "I often

wondered if I'd have to do it because of Carmella. I don't think I'm mentally strong enough to live my life out in the open without always looking over my shoulder. And then when the plea deal happened…" I shivered unexpectedly as my voice trailed off.

He nodded without saying a word.

"So, needless to say that once my ex came back into the picture, running away from everything sounded extremely appealing."

"Your parents would be worried sick."

"I'd let them know that I was okay."

"I wish I could tell you that I don't get it, but I do."

Surprise washed over me. "You do?"

"Absolutely. It's exhausting to think you can't just run to the grocery store without getting bothered or worrying that your ex is waiting for you at the house. Going into hiding makes perfect sense." He kept his gaze on me.

"Well, that's my secret. I've been fantasizing about it every day."

He took a sip of his club soda and set it down. I

felt a charge run between us as if this confession put a magnet right into my gut, and whatever there was about him pulled me right to him.

"I would miss you," he said.

"I would miss you too."

"Since we're sharing our secrets, I have one too."

My brows rose in surprise. "You do?"

He nodded. "Yeah. Right before you broke up with me, I'd gone to my brother about staying local more. We'd been toying around with an idea for a few years about building up a tactical facility here where we'd offer training to clients."

My heart skipped a beat as I nodded for him to continue.

"It was my way of being a better partner to you. I knew you needed me, and I should have listened more." He flagged down the server with a smile. "I think I'll have what she's having, too."

"Yes, sir." The server wandered off toward the bar as Zack brought his focus back to me.

"I'd planned on telling you everything, but you broke things off, and I knew if I told you what my plans had been, you wouldn't have trusted them. You would have thought I was throwing anything at the wall to see what stuck."

I chuckled, realizing he knew me too well.

"So, when this happened with Carmella, I offered my home to keep you secure." Zack let out a deep breath just as the server brought over his martini. He took a sip. "But my other intention was to win you back."

Chapter Eighteen

Zack

Her glassy eyes told me she'd been fighting back tears, and it killed me to think I did that to her. I never should have said what I said, but I also couldn't go on continuing like I didn't love her more than life itself. We had an amazing dinner, but the moment I'd told her my intentions, I could tell she'd put her walls back up.

Just when I thought we were making headway, I'd screwed it up.

I stared out my bedroom window as morning sunlight filtered through the glass, bathing my room in prisms of color.

A soft tap on my door made me straighten. I'd tried to avoid most people this morning by grabbing a cup of coffee and heading back up to my room, but I knew I needed to go downstairs and figure things out.

So far, Tim hadn't set foot anywhere near Sadie's parents, but that didn't solve the problem, which was Tim.

"It's Sadie," she said softly on the other side of the door.

My pulse quickened just from the thought of seeing her.

"Come on in," I said, smiling and turning around to see Sadie open the door.

Her hair was in a loose braid with all the fuzzy hairs on top from sleeping on it. She still had on a pair of pink satin boxers and a matching top. She looked dynamite as she held her own cup of coffee.

My stomach sank at the thought of all the mornings I wouldn't get to wake up seeing her in the future.

She grinned, setting her cup on my dresser. "I see

you snuck down and got some coffee."

"I'm sure it's God's gift to all of us non-morning people."

Her grin widened as she nodded. "Yet, you leap out of bed before five o'clock without a second thought to help people."

I nodded and took a sip of coffee. "I have no problem doing it. I'd prefer if problems in the world started around noon."

She laughed and came closer before sitting on my bed. I'd pulled up the navy blue comforter and fluffed the pillows up top, so the room looked somewhat decent. That had been one of her pet peeves, so I always tried to make the bed. Now, I just did it out of habit.

"So, what's up?" I looked at her over the rim of my mug.

"I couldn't sleep very well last night."

"I'm sorry. I never should have said what I did at dinner."

She shook her head and patted the place next to her. "No, I'm glad you did."

"You are?"

She let out a soft sigh and nodded. "Yeah, and it made me realize I'm tired of being scared. I'm done with it. It was a freak set of circumstances that led Carmella to me. I was nothing more than easy pickings for her, and it accomplished what she wanted. She got the attention of the Volkovs and my sister, the infamous crime blogger." Sadie looked at me. "And then my psycho first boyfriend was just another instance of bad luck, wrong place, wrong time, wrong person."

I studied her expression, wishing I knew where she was going with this.

"I wasn't even supposed to go out with Tim. He was expecting to meet my college roommate for a blind date, but she got sick and sent me."

I chuckled, shaking my head. "That is some bad luck."

Sadie smiled. "But I know my luck is turning around. I'm no longer going to let these people dictate how I want to spend my time on this earth. It took last night for me to realize that. When you told me what your plans were, it really hit home. I don't want to miss out on something or someone so special. I don't want to plan a life that is hidden from the people I care about."

"It would be devastating."

She nodded. "And saying my plan out loud last night made me really internalize what that meant."

I slid my hand on her leg, and she looked into my eyes. I felt the familiar charge between us as I imagined pulling her close and kissing her.

"I don't know how we're going to get through everything with Tim, but I want to believe there is a way to end it. And Carmella? I'll deal with it when the time comes. But until then, I'd like to be your first client at the training facility."

"You mean that?" I asked, tipping my chin.

It felt like the weight of the world had been lifted, but I knew we still had so much in front of us to get through.

But the thought of settling into a life with Sadie wasn't anything I'd let myself dare dream of since she'd broken things off.

She let out a deep breath and kicked her legs underneath her. "When you shared what happened about your parents and how that shared trauma didn't drive you and your brother away from one another, but it brought you closer, I realized how wrong I'd been." She shrugged. "I've been wrapping myself in a cloak of fear and worry, trying to run away from something that is impossible to run away from. And yet I had a man right next to me who made me feel... safe."

"Well, I wasn't always next to you, which was one of our issues," I offered with a smile.

"True, but I can't expect my partner to stay next to me twenty-four, seven."

"I wouldn't mind doing it."

She smiled and nodded as my phone buzzed. It was a message from Officer Carl, wanting to go over some stuff later. I clicked the message off and turned to face Sadie.

"Thanks for sticking with me even though I'm the most messed up creature on the planet."

"You're the strongest woman I've met who finally realized that your problems don't have to define you, and you certainly don't need to solve them yourself." I cupped her chin between my fingers as her mouth parted.

I slowly brushed my lips along hers, and she nipped my bottom lip playfully. This kiss could lead to so much more this morning. She parted her mouth, and so much emotion charged between us as our kisses turned hot and passionate. She slid her fingers through my hair as her breath hitched, and I tasted the sweetness of her lips. I wanted her again.

I needed her again.

And now, she might actually be mine.

Sadie's breathing changed as she crawled on my lap, wrapping her arms around my neck as she ground her hips into me.

She was pressed against my lap, and it would take a second before I got her pajamas off. She was so small compared to me, but she felt so large in this moment... as if she'd changed the entire trajectory of her life, her world. And it was so damn sexy.

Sadie pulled her mouth away as she stayed on my lap, her eyes fluttering open with a dopey grin sliding across her face.

"Thank you for that morning kiss." She slid off my lap, leaving me wanting her as she wiggled her hips.

I laughed, wiping my fingers across my lips as a twinkle lit up her gaze. "So, you were just bribing me with a little nookie?"

"Not exactly, but I'm feeling really… relieved. Now that the light of day is here, I can see things clearer. I spoke to my parents this morning, and they seem fine. My dad wants to get his hands around Tim's neck, I think." She laughed nervously. "And they encouraged me to try to live as normally as I can."

"Sounds good to me." I cupped my palms around her butt, and her smile melted my world into a sugary way of being.

"And since I won't be moving back there, I wondered if maybe we could visit… you know, after this thing with my ex is resolved."

She slid back on my lap and swept a kiss across my lips as I tried to shake the disturbing feeling racing through me.

"Absolutely."

"My sister and Jaxson said they were thinking about heading back tomorrow," she said softly, straightening on my lap.

"You'll miss her."

"I will."

I took a deep breath, unsure of what her answer would be. "Are you still thinking about heading back there?"

"Well, I sent everything back there, and I don't have my apartment any longer." Her lips fell into a fine line. "But I don't think a long-distance relationship is exactly what we need."

"And Tim is there."

"Yes, but apparently, he can get here too."

I nodded, feeling her frustration.

"But—"

"Will you move in with me, Sadie?"

"I kind of thought you'd never ask."

I held her close. "You mean just because I got dumped and thought you were going to run off to the Bahamas or Portugal that maybe I wanted to save an ounce of dignity?"

She giggled, and I held her close. "I think we've both been through enough that we can leave our egos at the door."

Sadie pressed her forehead against mine and smiled. "Thank you for giving me the space to figure out things. It's not that I feel completely better, but I sense hope. And I think that what I was missing this entire time was hope."

"I'll always try to give you what you need, Sadie." I slid my fingers down her messy braid.

"You do more than you know," she said softly. "But I should probably go spend some time with my sister before I meet Melanie for lunch."

"I think she's been waiting for me to get some common sense back." She flashed me a grin as she climbed off my lap. "She couldn't understand why on earth I broke up with you."

"I've always thought your sister was amazing."

She playfully rolled her eyes and walked out of my bedroom, and I wondered how my luck had turned around.

Chapter Nineteen

Sadie

It wasn't like I sprinkled magic fairy dust over my body and I suddenly wasn't scared any longer, but I woke up this morning knowing I couldn't keep living in fear.

Fear was what made me break up with Zack. Heartbreak.

Fear was what kept me quiet from telling anyone about Tim's first message. Embarrassment.

Fear of losing the man of my dreams. Isolation.

Fear of never being who I was meant to be.

Disgust.

But I was ready to tackle what life had in store for me. No more looking over my shoulder. No more hiding and being afraid of an old boyfriend who'd suddenly surfaced.

These things were manageable, not life-ending.

And Tim was nowhere on this side of the country.

I could at least enjoy these moments of peace and not push away the one stable force in my life.

I'd be lying to myself if I didn't admit I was still scared spitless. I was still worried that I'd open the door to see Tim staring back at me, but I didn't want to live in fear.

As Zack had said, my kidnapping was part of me. I couldn't expect to never think about it again or be triggered. Those things will happen, but it's how I navigate that trauma and frame it in my life that will make a difference, and that now includes Tim.

I flipped down the visor in Zack's Jeep and dotted on some lip gloss as I sat in front of Granite Beans.

Zack and his brother had been out in the woods discussing their future plans while Elena and Jaxson packed. It seemed like the perfect time to meet up with Melanie. She'd finally texted me, and I told her I'd love to meet her for lunch at Granite Beans.

The chill in the mountain air wrapped around me as I zipped my pink coat and made my way into the familiar coffee shop.

Melanie waved from behind the counter and quickly made her way over to me. She gave me a big squeeze, and I finally felt like maybe things were okay between us. Everything had been so screwed up in recent weeks that I didn't know if I was misreading things or if she was actually taking a few steps back.

"Have you heard anything else about the break-in?" I asked, hoping I didn't just set us backward.

She shook her head. "No, but the insurance company is waiting for some paperwork from the police, and I think that's it. I mean, I hope they figure out who it is, but at least I won't be out of pocket."

"Yeah, that whole thing wasn't what I expected to walk into that morning."

She nodded and gave me another squeeze, and I realized I hadn't even flinched either time.

Progress.

"I made your favorite sandwich. Basil and mozzarella," she said, walking to the small fridge behind the counter. "And I made turkey for me."

"Ah, I'm so spoiled." I touched my chest and batted my lashes as Melanie walked over with two plates piled high with a sandwich and chips on the side.

She set them down on the table and took a seat across from me.

"So, you're allowed out of the house now?" she teased.

"Something like that. Carmella is back in jail, and my ex-boyfriend isn't out here for the time being."

"Everything that's happened to you is absolutely... wild." Melanie picked up her sandwich and took a bite. "It's just... how much bad luck can one girl handle?"

I laughed and nodded. "I was beginning to ask myself that, too, but then it finally hit me that I didn't want to let other people dictate my happiness. I still want to be free to roam without looking over my shoulder, and somehow, I'll make that happen."

She reached over and squeezed my hand. "Good for you, Sadie. You deserve it."

"Thanks." I took a bite of chips and sat back in the chair. "So… how is it with Ian?"

A scowl fell across Melanie's features before she shrugged and smiled at me. "I don't know. It seems like it could be really complicated."

"Boys often are," I teased.

"This one especially." Melanie stood up. "I forgot the drinks. What do you want? A latte? Juice? Water?"

"I feel so bad being waited on. Anything will do."

Melanie grinned and grabbed us both a juice before going to the front door and locking it.

"You don't have to close the store for our lunch. I totally understand if someone comes in."

She waved her hand. "Nah. It's fine. It's been super slow today, and we have a lot to catch up on."

I nodded slowly. "Yeah, it feels like years have gone by."

"Your sister is so nice, and her husband is… wow."

"Yeah, they're a great couple."

Melanie nodded and took a bite of her sandwich. "They seemed like it."

Her eyes dropped to my plate. "Aren't you going to eat your sandwich?"

I chuckled, taking a sip of juice. "I'll eat every last morsel of it, don't you worry. So, tell me all about Ian."

"Well, he's cute. But he seems a little gullible."

My brows raised. "Gullible? That's a characteristic I wouldn't have guessed."

She shrugged. "Could just be me. I don't know. And he canceled on me when we had dinner planned."

I straightened in my chair and reached for a chip. "He did?"

That wasn't the story I'd heard.

"Yeah, so we'll see where it goes. I'm not holding my breath, and I have a business to grow."

"I understand that." I took a bite of the sandwich. "Have you hired someone else, or is my position still available?"

Her eyes widened. "Are you thinking about

staying?"

I nodded, taking another bite of the sandwich.

She clapped her hands together and grinned. "That is the best news ever."

"So I can have my job back?"

"It's always been yours, girl."

"I do have a question, though."

"What's up?"

"You know how you stopped by Zack's because you said you couldn't get ahold of me?"

"Yeah. What about it?"

"You never texted me."

She frowned and shook her head. "Sadie, I texted you."

"The next morning, Melanie. Not the night before."

"I don't know what you're getting at."

"I just wondered why you really stopped by."

"Are you okay, Sadie? You're freaking me out. Why wouldn't it be okay to stop by and check on a friend who's just found out that someone who's after her is now out of jail?"

I nodded. "No, no. You're right. That's completely normal. The right thing to do."

"Yeah. Exactly." Her eyes wouldn't meet mine, and I felt a cold sweat surface as I stared at this woman who'd always seemed so familiar to me. "Seriously, I'm kind of offended."

"Sorry. I didn't mean anything by it."

She tapped her finger on the table. "Just eat your sandwich. I think things are just getting to you, no matter what you think."

I took another bite and smiled at Melanie, but my mouth didn't feel like it was cooperating. My tongue felt thick and fuzzy as it twirled around the soft mozzarella. I reached for the juice and took a sip, trying not to panic.

"What's wrong, Sadie?" Melanie asked flatly.

Oh, no.

My gaze flashed to hers, and I tried to open my mouth to respond, but nothing happened. My mouth wouldn't move. My lips felt like pudding, sliding down my face.

The drink slipped from my fingers, spilling on the table.

Melanie glared at me. "Tsk, tsk. Now I have more to clean up."

"Mmm…" I tried so hard to speak. "Mmmone."

She stood, letting out a big sigh as my body slowly slouched out of the chair. "What was that? Call 9-1-1?"

I tried nodding, but she just stood staring at me.

"No, I think I have it handled."

A slow creep of pain slugged through my body as I stared at my friend, slowly making her way to the counter, where she grabbed a towel and drifted back to the table, where she leisurely wiped up the spilled liquid.

I tried again. "Mmm."

Her brows sharpened as she mimicked me. "Mmm."

My mouth wouldn't even open as my body drifted into a lifeless state. The heaviness of my lids made keeping my eyes open painful while my tongue swelled and my arms became frozen.

Melanie started humming as she cleaned, taking my sandwich plate away, but everything sounded like I was stuck underwater. The muffled taunts from my friend made my head spin between daggers. My head pounded as it lolled from side to side and I tried to ask for help.

And then the coughing. I couldn't stop, but it was like choking.

Every inhale turned to a spastic motion as I slithered from my seat. My arms failed to catch my convulsing body as my lungs felt engulfed in flames with every gasp of air.

As my body fell, I felt the coldness of the floor against my skin right before my head smacked the floor.

The pain was sharp and dug deep into my bones.

What had she done?

My head throbbed with every passing second, and my vision narrowed as I tried to watch the woman who was now dancing at my demise.

Tears slipped from my eyes as I tried to move.

But all I could do was stare blankly in front of me.

"You know, I ran into somebody the other day around town. You might know him. Tim is his name."

My body stiffened in pain, but I could do nothing.

"Actually, I'm not being entirely honest. I don't just know him. He's my brother, but I wouldn't expect you to know that. You're such a self-absorbed little brat."

Panic drilled into me as she knelt in front of me, wiping the tears from my face and licking them.

"You still don't remember me, do you?" She sank lower, narrowing her eyes on me. "You were always so obsessed with yourself. How does it feel now?" She let out a deep breath and stood, crossing her arms over her chest. "You're pathetic, and now it's your turn to pay for what you did to my brother."

"Mmm," My body writhed in desperation as she stared at me.

Her red hair and fair eyebrows had been replaced with brunette coloring, and dread filled me slowly.

Familiarity blazed through me as my mind transformed the woman in front of me.

"He had to give up his dreams because your prick of a father got the police involved. Oh, don't look surprised. You didn't actually believe the reason my brother stayed away was because your dad was so big and strong, did you?"

Her steady eyes stayed on me, taking it all in as if she couldn't wait to report back to her brother.

"He stayed away until the time was right, and Carmella only made things easier, and then came the fame. You must have loved every second, your image blazed across the newspapers and magazines with Zack carrying you out from the warehouse—like you're a damsel in distress." She laughed. "My brother knew you'd be dumb enough to fall for your hero, so he sent me out here and had me buy out this coffee shop just to set this up. Gave me the funds to make the offer too good to be true." An evil grin twisted on her lips. "And my generous brother gave me enough extra to seal my lips and play along."

I never should have left without telling anyone.

Zack will find me.

He'd know after an hour or two that something was wrong.

He'd be here.

"My brother loved you. He worshiped you, and you destroyed his spirit. Do you know what that's like?"

I tried to nod.

"And then you stopped messaging me, as if I had some plague?" She spat on my leg. "You little bitch."

She pulled zip ties from her apron and knelt, cinching them around my wrists and ankles so tightly it took my breath away. She hovered over me and took a photo.

"Tim will be thrilled to see this. He made me promise not to interrupt him until he was through with your parents, but I think he'll love it." She cocked her head slightly as she saw the horror surface in my eyes.

My parents.

"That's right, princess. My brother thought it was only fair that we teach your dad a lesson. You know, the way he felt the need to teach one to Tim. But all in good time. I'm getting ahead of myself. I love this, though. I've been tiptoeing around here and walking on eggshells, laughing at your ridiculous jokes, listening to you fawn over your hero. It has been exhausting."

She stalked over and smiled. "I wonder what your boyfriend will do when he realizes he couldn't save you just like he couldn't save his parents."

Her hand came at me, grabbing my hair as she hit me hard enough to make the room spin. I tried keeping my eyes open, but darkness fell.

And the silence was deafening.

Chapter Twenty

Zack

"Sadie?" I charged through the house. "Sadie?"

I darted through the halls upstairs and went downstairs to the mudroom. The key to the Jeep was missing. I threw open the garage door to see the empty spot in the garage.

Was this morning all pretend? Had she been planning this the entire time? To vanish?

"Elena?" I hollered, rushing to the kitchen. "Did

Sadie tell you where she was going?"

I started texting Sadie.

No reply.

I called her, holding the phone to my ear.

No answer.

She scowled. "Going? She was upstairs last I checked."

"Sadie took the Jeep." I punched the granite counter. "Damn it. I knew it was too good to be true."

"We'll find her," Elena promised. "But what was too good to be true?"

"She'd changed her tune with me. We were going to start a future, visit your parents. She was going to move in." I clenched my fists, ignoring the throbbing in my fingers.

"I gotta find her before she leaves town."

"Zack, she loves you. My sister's not going anywhere. Maybe she just needed to feel a little bit of freedom again."

I nodded as my brother came into the room.

"Sadie and my Jeep are gone."

Ian nodded, and Officer Carl just texted and

wanted us to meet him at the station.

Panic filled me.

I looked at Elena and took a deep breath. "Get Jaxson and meet us at the station."

"Will do." Terror filled her gaze. "Tim is still in New England, right?"

"As far as I know." I nodded. "Jaxson confirmed it earlier."

I followed Ian out the door, hopping into his dually truck. The tension in the air amplified when he pulled onto the main road to the police station.

"What was she thinking?" I bobbed my knee up and down as I stared mindlessly out the window.

"It's going to be fine, Zack. She's probably just getting some fresh air. Tim isn't here. Let her live a little. You know you won't be able to do this soon, right?"

My gaze snapped to him. "Do what?"

"Keep her on a leash?"

I stared at my phone, watching the security footage of Sadie driving away in my Jeep.

His words washed through me, and I realized the reality of the situation. "No, you're right. I'm probably overreacting. She's not in danger. No reason to panic."

But my gut told me something else.

"Exactly. All the facts point to her just going to town for a quick trip."

I let out a slow breath, unsure of whether I wanted to tell my brother about her confession to me, about how she wanted to vanish.

The police department came into view, and Ian parked close to the front door. There weren't many cars in the lot, which wasn't a surprise. Not a lot of things happened in a small mountain town.

As we made our way up to the front door, a chill skittered over me. I glanced behind me, but I only saw my brother.

We entered the spacious lobby, and Officer Carl poured himself a cup of coffee.

"Thanks for stopping by. Grab a cup of coffee if you'd like," Officer Carl said, waving us into his office. "Sometimes, it's just easier to have a good-old-fashioned chat rather than texts, and emails, and voicemails."

We walked by the coffee station straight into his office.

"Yeah, I'm interested to hear what you've got," I told him.

My brother took a seat next to me.

"Well, I have more than I expected to tell. You know, something struck me as odd about the video from the night of the break-in. Something familiar."

I nodded, propping my elbows on my knees while I leaned forward. I knew Officer Carl always liked a good story, but I needed to find Sadie.

"Tell me more."

"And I can now say with near one hundred percent certainty that the person on the video was Melanie."

I couldn't hide my shock. "Melanie? She owns the place. Are you talking insurance fraud or…"

Officer Carl nodded. "I believe so. I had to turn everything over to the proper authorities because that type of crime changes jurisdictions, and then one can of worms after another opened"

"What do you mean?"

"Well, her real name isn't Melanie."

My mind spun with his words, tangling a messy

web of deceit that sank deep into my soul.

I had failed. How did I not see through her façade?

A cold chill ran through my body as I bolted from my seat.

I eyed Officer Carl. "Is her real name Tracy?"

Ian stood next to me.

Officer Carl nodded. "I'll be. It sure is."

"Last name Venson." Ian shook his head.

I was out the door.

"Where you headed?" Officer Carl called after us.

"We have to find Sadie," Ian shouted as we dashed out of the station.

My pulse pounded heavily as I slid out my phone, texting Jaxson.

"No, no, no…" I muttered, popping my knuckles as we climbed into his truck.

"For the first time ever, I hope Sadie took off and left us all behind."

Ian eyed me as he turned on the truck. "But you know she didn't, man. You know she didn't."

"Get to Granite Beans," I told him.

He nearly squealed out of the lot, glancing at me. "I noticed you didn't invite the officer."

"I'm tired of doing things clean, Ian. I'm done."

"We'll find her."

Within minutes, Granite Beans came into view, and so did my Jeep.

"Shit."

"It's fine. She's going to be fine, Zack."

But I could feel it.

Sadie wasn't fine. She'd needed me, and I failed her.

Just like I failed my parents.

Ian pulled behind the Jeep, and I jumped out before he'd even turned the engine off. Racing to Granite Beans' door, I pulled on it to find it locked.

"Shit."

Ian came up behind me.

"It's locked." My heart was beating so fast that I felt dizzy. I pressed my face to the glass, seeing no one inside.

"I'll go around back," Ian said.

I straightened and breathed as my brother jogged away, and I kicked into the glass. It shattered instantly as I reached my hand inside and twisted the deadbolt. A piece of glass shredded my knuckle, but I didn't care. I stepped inside, spotting a table with one juice bottle turned on its side and the other upright.

"Sadie?" I shouted, racing to the backroom.

Empty.

My brother pounded on the back door as I ran over to open it.

"She's not here."

He nodded, holding up her phone. "This was on the pavement by the back door."

Fury raced through my veins. These people would pay.

"Hey, Zack, Ian," Jaxson's voice boomed through the coffee shop. "We've got problems."

I turned around to see a look of horror washing over Elena's face as Jaxson's eyes met mine.

"Tim subdued my people, and he's got their parents tied up. He sent a video message."

The room spun around me.

How was this possible?

How did a weasel outsmart so many of us?

"My brothers' ETA is less than ten minutes. The situation should be handled quickly at that point. Blake and Devin know what they're doing. It's family." He eyed me. "No authorities will be involved."

Jaxson was no longer asking for permission, but I would have gladly given it.

I nodded as Ian glanced at me.

"Affirmative." I nodded. "They've got Sadie."

"Who has Sadie? Tim isn't here," Elena whispered, covering her mouth.

"His sister, Melanie. Her real name is Tracy."

Elena looked like she was going to be sick. "Tracy Venson."

I nodded, taking a deep breath. I had to focus. "We'll find her."

My heart thundered inside my chest as I shoved away the terror racing through me.

Forgive me, Sadie. I will find you.

I reached for her phone, entering the code as my mind raced with options. These people liked to play games. They liked to taunt and torment.

What was it he'd always call her?

Little seashell?

And then it clicked. Tim hadn't been here to set up the mementos in her apartment. That must have been Tracy, and the seashell left in Sadie's room? That was her, too. Sadie just hadn't noticed it until a few days later.

"How did I miss the signs?" I banged my fist against the wall as a message popped up on Sadie's phone.

My little seashell, I hope you understand how surprised your parents were to see me. I look forward to sending you footage of our little welcome party. How's my sister treating you? Well, I hope. Enjoy the accommodations that I booked for you two. They'll be your last. ~Tim

"She's still alive." I eyed Ian. "But I don't know for how long. I don't think Tim realizes she doesn't have her phone. He's planned for his sister to take her somewhere."

Elena's eyes stayed on mine, and I didn't want to say the rest aloud. I handed the phone to my brother, and Jaxson came over to look at the screen.

I would not fail Sadie.

We would find her in time.

I walked out front, scanning the room for any clues. Opening the lid on the trash, I saw a half-eaten mozzarella sandwich. Sadie's favorite. I lifted it from the trash and opened it up, seeing small granules stuck to the tomato. That wasn't salt.

Tracy had drugged her.

My chest clenched as I rifled through the trash until I finally found a crumpled piece of paper.

Sickness pulsed through me at an unstoppable rate. I knew I was going to be ill any second. I dashed to the sink, spitting into it as I uncrumpled the paper and scanned two words.

Seaside Motel.

"I've got a possible lead. Seaside Motel over on Granite Lake."

"That dump?" Ian asked, coming to my side. "Hasn't it been closed for a couple of years?"

I nodded. "Perfect place to go unseen. We don't have time."

Jaxson typed the place into his phone. "No, we don't."

He turned to Elena. "You stay here."

Elena nodded, hugging herself as we all barreled out of Granite Beans.

Sadie had every right to always look over her shoulder. Evil nipped at her every move, and she knew it. She just didn't understand it.

What kind of depraved person would do this? Over an old college relationship?

And his sister?

This kind of depravity ran deep. It wasn't easily stopped.

We climbed into my brother's truck, and he jerked it to life. I held onto the oh-shit bar as he did a U-turn in the middle of town and raced down the road toward the old motel.

"ETA for my brothers arriving on scene at their

parents' is less than five minutes."

"Shit." I shook my head. "Tim is a showman. He's been waiting for this moment. He wants to embarrass and torture her parents in front of her."

Ian's grip tightened around the wheel. "And then when that's over with, she'll be of no use to him."

"Exactly," I agreed as the horror of the situation wove its way through me.

"We'll get there in time," Jaxson said from behind us.

He was staring at his phone, and I wasn't sure he believed it.

Chapter Twenty-One

Sadie

My head pounded with a sharpness that made my stomach sick. My wrists burned from the plastic ties digging into my skin.

But I was alive.

A low hum vibrated through me as I opened my eyes and looked around, trying to figure out where she had taken me.

"You're up. Just in time," Tracy cooed.

"Wheremmm..." I tried to speak.

"Shh. Come now. Don't waste your words. Save

them for my brother."

I looked around the tiny room, realizing the hum I heard was a generator out the back.

Seashells had been strung along the ceilings. Stained wallpaper coated the walls around me. A large flatscreen had been hung in front of me, completely out of step with the condition of the room. My stomach clenched. This had been planned for a long time.

I wiggled to my side. She'd put me on a dirty mattress with a few blankets on top.

Please, Zack. I'm so sorry for leaving without telling. I'm in a motel.

It was my fault.

"So, it's close to showtime. My brother just needed a little extra prep time. Turns out your dad had a bit of a fight in him after all." She laughed wickedly as my stomach roiled with sickness.

"Lvhmln," I screamed.

"What was that? Leave him alone?" Her laughter continued. "I might have sprinkled a little too much on your sandwich. I think Tim wanted you to be able to talk with him."

Tracy frowned. "But I can only do so much. I can't tell you how aggravating it was to pretend to be your friend. Ich." She pretended to shiver. "Anyway, we have quite the show planned for you."

Her phone buzzed, and she looked down at the screen, smiling.

"It's time."

I tried to sit up, but my head hurt too much, and the way my wrists had been bound made it impossible.

Tracy turned on the television. Brightness from the images on the screen filled the room as my world turned to terror.

My parents were tied to chairs in their own kitchen while Tim paced back and forth. He stopped and slowly raised a blade to my mom's cheek, tracing it across her flesh.

The terror of what was before me nearly paralyzed me. But I had something I hadn't held for a long time.

Hope.

Tim turned around and faced the camera, ducking down. His head became larger than life, and I winced.

He looked exactly like I remembered, only more sadistic.

And small, weak, and narcissistic.

That grin was so knowing, welcoming the pain he was about to inflict.

"Don't do what he says, Sadie. We'll be fine," my dad called out.

Tim whipped around and slapped my father's cheek. "Shut up, old man."

My jaw ached. "Lvmfalone."

Tim spun around, looking into the camera. "Oh, really? What are you going to do about it, Sadie? You want me to leave your daddy alone?"

I spat at the camera angled directly at me.

Damn it. I wished I could speak more clearly. The brain fog was lifting every second, but my mouth wouldn't cooperate.

My dad stared directly into the camera at me. I could feel his strength. He wouldn't go without a fight.

"I'm all for family reunions, but we should get things started." Tim's smile turned into a toothy grin as he adjusted the camera slightly. "Let's start with your faithful wife. Shall we?"

"Mmmom." I got the word out. "I love you."

My mom's smile brightened the screen. "We love you too, Sadie."

It was as if those words gave me the strength I needed.

Tim stretched his arm wide and started to swing, but before he could land the punch, a loud crash sounded through the video.

My eyes searched the screen for any clues. Tim still stood in front of my mother, but he was frozen. A loud thud echoed, and breaking glass reverberated through the speakers as Tracy gasped.

Two masked, faceless men entered the room. They towered over Tim and my parents.

Heavily armed.

Tim lunged at one of them with a knife while the other took direct aim.

Bang.

One shot.

Tracy screamed as her brother crumpled to the floor. The camera captured everything as tears slowly fell down his sister's cheeks.

"My daughter. My daughter," my mom screamed as Tracy knelt in front of the television, crying. "Help her."

I wiggled over to Tracy, trying to kick her in the head with my feet, but that only made her bolt upright.

I glanced at the screen as the video turned off, and I knew my parents were saved. They'd gotten to them in time, but those two men...

Who I knew well...

I wasn't so sure of my own fate.

They spared my parents from watching what might unfold.

The horror slammed into me like a freight train.

"You've taken away the one person who's ever loved me," Tracy seethed. Her breathing was like an animal's as she hovered over me. "I will make you pay."

She licked her lips as if she were rabid. This was not the woman I knew.

But now I couldn't unsee the Tracy before me. How had I not recognized Melanie as her?

Tracy walked over to a box. She bent over it as I tried to worm my way off the mattress.

"Where do you think you're going?" Tracy's eyes flashed to mine. "I have a promise to keep to my brother."

"What's that?" My words still slurred, but they weren't so useless.

"That you would help feed the seashells of the world." Her eyes blackened as she bent back over the box. "This one should do well. This one, too."

I slinked like a snake toward the door, only feet away.

I could do this. Maybe someone would see me.

Tracy straightened and laughed. "Where do you think you're going?"

Holding a knife in each hand, she let out a tearful sigh. "Ah, so much better. I felt a little vulnerable before, if you know what I mean."

She put one of the knives in her other hand and wiped away a stray tear.

Maybe there was some way to get through to her. She could get help. She didn't have to ruin the rest of her life.

"The brother you know today was the one I knew I needed to get away from years ago. He was a bad man, Tracy. But that doesn't mean you are too." I stared at her, my head slouching against the wall.

If I could somehow prop myself just right, I could reach the doorknob.

And just get outside.

"What do you know? You dumped him and never looked back." She shook her head. "I thought he'd almost forgotten about you." She clanked the knives together. "But then you got yourself in the news. The moment my brother saw the way you looked at Zack, he came unglued."

"That doesn't make it right. You don't have to keep going, Tracy."

"It's too late, Sadie. I'm already in this, and now, with my brother gone, I have nothing left to lose."

"Your freedom. They'll find you." I stared at her, unable to understand how she had so much hate for me. "You will pay for this."

"Just like your Carmella?" She laughed as a prickle of terror ran through my spine. "Do you know how awful our childhood was, Sadie? Did you ever stop to listen to what Tim and I went through growing up?"

I cleared my throat and shook my head. "I asked about his family a lot, but he'd never let me in. He'd never tell me about your parents or how you grew up. I only met you in person once."

Her brows rose. "So, what's your excuse? I wasn't worthy of friendship because we'd only met once. What about all those messages day and night for over a year? We talked about everything."

"We didn't talk about everything. I don't know about your family."

I knew I needed to buy time. It was my only chance at surviving this.

Time was my hope.

"Why don't you tell me about them?"

She took two steps and stood over me, glaring with her knives. "They didn't care about us. How about that?"

"Tell me more." I kept my eyes steady on hers.

Tracy crouched down, and we were eye-to-eye. I could smell a hint of fear on her breath as she let out a sigh. She wasn't entirely certain about doing the next step.

"They beat my brother until he couldn't walk because he killed his goldfish." She stared at the wall. "It wasn't his fault. He didn't mean to."

"I'm sure he didn't."

"That was the first time it happened. When his guinea pig died, they did it too. He could barely walk."

I swallowed down the shock registering through me.

"Did he have issues with animals, Tracy?"

She shrugged, bringing her blade to my cheek. "Not like I did."

A chill hung in the air as I kept my eyes focused on hers. The cold blade scraped against my flesh as she smiled. "I remember one morning, there was this bird that wouldn't shut up. Just chirp. Chirp. Chirp." She laughed. "I couldn't handle it."

My throat clenched with fear.

"I never heard it chirp again."

"Did you enjoy that, Tracy?"

She smirked. "Very much. Probably more than

Tim. He enjoyed the slow taunting, like using AI to send you voicemails and calls from Carmella. That was priceless."

The reality of her words hit me hard. It had never been Carmella leaving voicemails and calling. It had been Tim, but I couldn't show my surprise. I had to keep focused. Drag this out.

"And what about your parents?" I asked as my throat turned to sandpaper.

"I think they enjoyed hurting us, if that's what you're asking. But they got what was coming to them."

The realization that time might not be on my side worked through my body as Tracy stood and walked over to the window. She pulled back a dusty curtain and peeked outside.

"Life works in mysterious ways." She took a step back from the curtain, letting it swing as she hummed a tune I didn't understand. "There was a part of me that thought your boyfriend might find you, but I guess luck is on my side."

"Do you miss your brother?" I asked, keeping my voice steady.

"Miss him? Hmm. Miss what he promised me? Yes. Miss him? No. Maybe not." She laughed, turning to look at me. "He wasn't a nice guy."

She lifted the knives again and smiled.

"I've gathered that."

Tears stung my eyes as I closed my eyes and willed the pain to go away. I would not show weakness to this predator.

But every single part of my body hurt.

"Why did you go along with what your brother wanted to do?" I asked, genuinely curious.

"Money."

I nodded, surprised at the simplicity of it all.

Behind me, I heard the crunch of wheels on the gravel parking lot.

I stared straight ahead, praying I wouldn't give away a thing.

An engine idled and shut off.

Tracy hadn't seemed to notice.

I drew a breath as she locked her gaze on mine and lunged forward.

Chapter Twenty-Two

Zack

Every mile felt like ten.

"My brothers got in. The mission is complete."

Relief spread through me. At least when we got to Sadie, we could give her some good news.

We would get to Sadie.

Jaxson sighed heavily. "But we've lost visual confirmation of Sadie."

My pulse spiked. "What do you mean?"

"She's alive as of thirty seconds ago." Jaxson's voice was determined but emotionless.

Anger pulsed through me. "Is that supposed to make me feel better?"

"Why can't they see her?" I pressed, watching a blur of pine and fir trees speed by.

"They cut the video," Jaxson answered.

"Why would they do that?"

"Several reasons."

I shook my head in anger.

"You wanted to do things our way, Zack."

I turned in the seat to look at Jaxson.

His eyes stayed on mine. "We don't get caught, and we will continue operating like that."

I nodded. "No. I get it."

"There it is," Ian said as the dumpy motel came into view.

The L-shaped, one-story building had about a dozen doors. The white paint on the building had long since turned beige. The lime green doors now looked like the color of split-pea soup.

I scoured every inch of the building and spotted a curtain ruffling in the distance.

"There. Three doors from the left end." We'd

found the right room. Ian parked the truck by the road. I jumped out, racing toward the pea-green door. I would make it in time.

I would save Sadie if it were the last thing I did.

Ian and Jaxson were right behind me.

My chest tightened with each strained breath as I reached that door.

I kicked it in, the door smacking into the wall as Tracy towered over Sadie under the window. Her knives raised, she roared like an animal as the blades dove toward Sadie's chest.

I tackled Tracy down onto a dirty mattress, and she rolled out from under me. She sprang up as Ian came into the room. Her eyes widened as she looked at Sadie.

She was primal. Her eyes filled with primitive rage, and I knew this wasn't her first kill.

Ian reached for Sadie with Jaxson's help to move her to safety.

I locked my arm around Tracy's throat, bringing her down to the mattress and pressing her into a neck crank. She popped back up.

The dirty mattress beneath my boots sent shivers

up my spine. I couldn't believe this was where Sadie had been kept.

But I kept my focus unwavering. I was dealing with crazy. I locked eyes with Tracy. She wasted no time and stepped forward, attempting to mirror my movements.

She'd had training. She wielded her knives with a chilling expertise. My right hand gripped her collar while my left hand snatched her sleeve. She tried to pull guard, but I dropped my weight down, hoping to evade her technique before she could establish her next move.

But she was quick, and the sharpness of her knife sliced into my thigh as her spine turned rigid from the spinal lock.

Sadie's eyes met mine with a gasp when she saw my wound.

Tracy wasted no time and stepped in to prove her skill quickly. I mirrored Tracy's movements, getting a solid ribbon grip with my right hand while my left hand seized her arm. But she was quick and managed to lock a closed guard around my waist. The pressure of her legs, trying to break my stance, surprised me. The pain in my thigh throbbed as a constant trickle of warm liquid dribbled down my leg. But I postured up just as she attempted a triangle choke. I couldn't help but admire her abilities, but it was over.

Recognizing the danger immediately, I stacked her to prevent the chokehold from getting tighter. She crumpled to the ground and coughed but stood back up with her remaining knife. I had no plans to end her, and I knew Ian felt the same. I kept my knife sheathed.

Jaxson, I didn't believe, did.

Tracy's eyes skittered up and down my body as a smile curled across her lips. "Leg looks pretty bad."

"Could be worse."

This took her off-guard, and she quickly realized her mistake.

I tackled her to the mattress. Breathing heavily as the pain in my thigh roared to life, I shifted my weight and managed to transition my good knee onto her belly, digging into her abdomen. She gasped from the pain.

Her eyes blazed with hate as she gripped the other knife and shoved it toward me. The silver of the blade flashed in the light as her fingers tightened around the blade.

And I had no choice.

Her body went lifeless as the knife fell from her hands, which had only slightly scraped my shoulder.

"Get me free. Get me free," Sadie cried, grabbing at one of the knives.

"I got you, Sadie," I said, working the blade through the plastic tie around her ankles.

The pain from my thigh made me wince as the knife dropped from my hand. I only had enough strength to undo her first restraint.

Shit. This wasn't good.

She gasped as she tripped toward me, looping her locked wrists around me and bringing me into her.

"You saved me," she whispered through tears. "Again."

I looked into her eyes and smiled, feeling my pulse slow with every beat. "It's over, baby. I knew it would be, but it's really over."

Sadie sniffled as Jaxson bent over, slicing the tie around her wrist. Ian was applying a tourniquet as Jaxson paced outside.

"Call 9-1-1," Sadie cried. "Just call an ambulance."

Ian knelt next to me, keeping his eyes on my injury.

Jaxson brought the truck to the door.

"Why aren't you calling the medics?" she nearly screamed.

"Keeping you safe and my brother and the Volkovs out of trouble is more important," I said as confidently as I could.

"No. No. No. No. Don't say that." She beat her fist on my chest. "I need you."

Her voice went distant. "I'm here, Sadie. I'll always be here."

Jaxson and Ian lifted me to the truck, sliding me into the backseat. Sadie wouldn't leave my side. Jaxson shut the door and climbed into the truck as Ian peeled out of the parking lot.

"Let's just pray that no one drives by until help arrives," Jaxson muttered.

"Help?" Sadie questioned through tears. "Aren't we getting Zack help?"

"He means help to clean up the scene."

My eyes met Sadie's, and I wondered if this was the end.

Coldness fell over me as I tried to lift my fingers to hers.

She was so beautiful. She was worth it all. She was worth everything.

I smiled at her, and she wiped away a tear, leaving a smudge of blood in its place.

"We need the hospital." Sadie's gaze hardened. "And I don't care who goes to jail."

"I'm getting him there, Sadie. I wouldn't let my brother…"

His words sounded muffled, like I was in some emotionless nightmare where I wanted to holler, but nobody heard.

Sadie leaned over me, her familiar scents of coconut and lime washing over me.

Man, I loved this woman.

I'd do anything for her.

"ETA is three minutes," Jaxson supplied.

Did I have three minutes? I closed my eyes as

Sadie ran her fingers down my cheek.

"You've got this, Zack. We've got plans. We've got our future. Don't you die on me. I will be so pissed."

I tried to laugh, but I just flicked my eyes open, trying to take in every second of her that I could before...

Jaxson was on the phone speaking in some code, or I was even farther gone than I realized. He hung up and looked at my brother. Both of their expressions were grim. There were no pep talks.

"Things should be taken care of in less than thirty," Jaxson explained.

Ian scowled. "How is that even possible?"

Jaxson nodded. "Do you want answers?"

Ian shook his head. "No, but thank you. You're right. Less is better."

"Call my sister," Sadie said softly as her thumb gently caressed my forehead.

"I've texted her, and she's taking the Jeep to the hospital. She'll be there when we arrive."

Sadie slowly nodded, and I realized she knew what I'd just realized.

I wasn't going to make it.

Chapter Twenty-Three

Sadie

One Year Later

Everything reminded me of Zack Parker as I walked through the woods at his house. The autumn chill in the air skated across my skin as I breathed in the sweet smell of maple leaves. I stopped at the tree where he'd kissed me so tenderly last year.

The turning point.

I bent down, picked up a scarlet leaf, and closed my eyes, breathing in the cold air and feeling closer to

Zack than ever.

That moment when I realized that I wanted more. I needed more. I had to stop blaming my traumatic past for my chaotic future. That moment was right here in Zack's arms as his lips touched down to mine.

And it was Zack who showed me what bravery could create.

A new world.

New beginnings.

I realized I couldn't blame the man who carried me out of the storm and into the light. He was my light.

My therapist was very wrong.

He didn't remind me of the bad event. He represented the good in the world. He always had.

Zack Parker had always been the man who was meant to show me what love could be and how it should be.

I was just blinded by my own history to see it until it was almost too late.

And I was so grateful for the time I had with Zack. He showed me so much during a time when I thought my life and my freedom had ended forever.

I let out a wistful sigh as I walked through the woods to a clearing at the base of a large hill.

This had been my secret dream. The one I knew I should never voice because of how ridiculous it sounded. And then I told Zack, and he believed in me.

In the vision.

And he had one of his own.

"I'll never let you go, Zack Parker. Your heart is always with mine," I whispered, letting the leaf float to the ground as I made my way down the hill.

A six-month-old golden retriever yapped in the distance, circling a newly fenced pasture. A red barn erected at the end of the property had an empty ladder propped on the edge, the last of the white trim being painted.

The last of Zack's and my dreams melded into one.

If only…

"Come here, Sugar Beans," I hollered at the puppy.

The golden retriever clumsily galloped on his oversized paws in the grass in a desperate attempt to run toward me. She knew I always had a piece of cheese.

I bent down as Sugar Beans dove into me, pushing me over. I laughed so hard as her cold, slick tongue smacked my cheek as my feet kicked in the air.

"Hey now, Sugar Beans. That's my job right there. Don't get it twisted." Zack's voice boomed through the air as my giggling got worse.

He pulled Sugar Beans off me and put out his hands for me. "I swear you're more gorgeous than when you left for school this morning."

"You're just trying to get me to lick you like Sugar Beans." I chuckled as he pulled me into his arms.

Zack closed the gap between us instantly. "Is that a bad thing?" His mouth nestled into the crook of my neck, and he breathed in.

"I missed you," he said softly. "These classes are brutal."

I nodded, feeling the strength of his body holding me tight.

It was moments like this when I knew it was all worth it, the nights away in Seattle while I finished my degree and traveled back on the weekends. The nights we slept in our separate beds while I crashed from studying too much. But thankfully, my classes were Tuesdays and Thursdays, so I had Friday through Monday back in Granite Peak.

"Mmm, you feel so good next to me, baby." His hands slid from my back to my head, his fingers moving through my hair. "Good to see you again."

His hazel eyes locked on mine, and I couldn't help but smile.

"I missed you," I muttered, feeling weak in the knees just being next to him.

Zack bent down and kissed me. His warm lips pressed against mine, sending a buzz of anticipation for what awaited me this weekend. I parted my lips as his tongue tasted me. He let out a little groan of satisfaction before Sugar Beans jumped on us, barking.

I chuckled as his mouth parted from mine. "I hope there's more of that tonight."

"I still can't believe you named our first puppy together after Granite Beans," he joked.

"Hey, you taught me to turn sour things into something sweet, and Sugar Beans is the sweetest there is."

His gaze smoldered as he took a step back. Zack's low-slung jeans made my heart skip a beat as he stretched toward the sky with the sixty-pound retriever in his hands like she was as light as a paperweight.

"Who's a good girl? Who's my Sugar Beans?" he asked, putting her back on the ground.

She took off toward the barn.

"It looks incredible," I said, taking a step closer.

"I'm glad we went with red."

"Me too. It really looks awesome this time of year too."

He looped his arm around my waist and brought me in tighter.

"How's your leg?" I asked, leaning my head on his shoulder.

"It's a leg." He laughed, shaking his head.

"Are you sure you should really be up on that ladder?" I asked, turning to face him.

"You ask me that after I framed and built the entire barn?"

I grinned. "Well, when you put it that way, I

guess one last time on a ladder isn't that big of a deal."

He swept a kiss across my forehead and smiled. "Do you ever stop worrying?"

"Nope, but isn't that why you love me?"

"Among the reasons," he said, tangling his fingers with mine.

"Want to take a seat on a hay bail?" I asked. "These boots are all for being cute, but not actually booting."

He chuckled. "Booting?"

"Official term."

Zack grinned wider. "I love you so much, Sadie Egorov."

I laughed. "Phew, because I've put you through a lot. Possibly more than most."

He laughed and brought me into him as we walked over to a place to sit as the sun went down.

"I wouldn't change it for the world, Sadie. Not one second."

"Not even one physical therapy session?" I teased, knowing how much work he'd put in to be where he was today.

His eyes stayed on mine. "No, because you were there with me on every single one of them."

My heart filled with so much love I almost didn't know what to do or say.

"I love you so much, Zack. I just… I'm so sorry I put you through that uncertainty. I just…"

"Sadie, you never have to apologize to me. We got where we were meant to be."

"I thought I was going to lose you that day," I whispered, looking into his eyes.

"Then we're even." He kept his gaze on me. "The thought of living in this world without you seemed like a death sentence on its own."

He kept his fingers looped through mine. "You have to promise me a few things, Sadie."

I turned to face him and tucked my leg underneath me. "Yeah? Like what?"

Zack's mouth curled into a delicious smile. "Lots of babies. Lots of dogs. A few horses. Maybe a dozen goats. A few chickens."

I laughed. "Are you the same Zack Parker from Granite Peak Security? The one who'd leave for weeks at a time to go fight the bad guys?"

He smiled and scooped me onto his lap. "I'm ready to start helping the good guys, Sadie. Your dream is my dream."

My chest filled with such adoration for this man.

This big, burly man.

With the heart of a tender chipmunk.

"What's that goofy look for?" he asked, etching his thumb against my brow.

"Just picturing you as a chipmunk."

He cocked his head slightly and laughed. "Should I be worried? I wasn't quite ready for this phase of the relationship."

I chuckled and let out a deep breath before resting my head on his chest.

"You're my everything, Zack Parker. Forever and more." I lifted my head. "Thank you for saving me from myself."

Chapter Twenty-Four

Zack

Having Sadie in my arms felt like all the worries of the world no longer mattered. She was here. She was mine.

Lines were crossed that I never imagined, but sometimes, love makes you realize what's worth fighting for.

And Sadie was worth it all.

She wiggled on my lap as the sun went down as slowly as it rose.

The fiery sun, with its golden orb over the

horizon, brushed the clouds with subtle hues of orange, pink, and lavender. It felt like the world had been holding its breath for this moment. The breeze had stilled, only leaving the sweet smell of leaves to drift around us.

Sadie wore a simple plaid shirt dress that fluttered playfully over her lap as she scooted on mine. Her long, dark hair cascaded into a simple braid tied with a matching red ribbon. I couldn't help but fall in love with her a little more as her full mouth swept across my lips.

I didn't want to rush tonight. It would only happen once, and every second of it mattered to me.

Sugar Beans barked in the distance as the last of the light drifted to a quiet darkness.

Sadie lifted her head from my chest and let out a deep sigh. "Beautiful sunset, as always."

I nodded, taking her in. "Think about our future often?"

"All the time," she said softly, smiling. "I know without a doubt that you're my future."

"And this is all for us." I squeezed her gently. "I'm so proud of you, Sadie. It's not easy to go back to school."

"I'm just lucky they took my first two years. I only have a year left and then nine months for the certification. No biggie." She waggled her brows. "When I have you to come home to on the weekend."

She rolled her hips into me, and I cupped her butt. "Damn, girl. You're making things tough right now."

Sadie giggled and smiled. "Do you have something in mind for our future I should know about?"

My heart raced, and my palms got clammy. This was the moment I'd been waiting for since I woke up in the hospital.

Sadie was the first person I saw. She was the first person to tell me how much she loved me.

And how mad she was at me. The thought made me chuckle.

My eyes opened to see Sadie's beautiful face searching mine for recognition, and the moment I smiled, she squealed and leaned in to kiss me.

It was the most beautiful thing in this world.

Until tonight.

Tonight was going to be magical.

"I've been thinking about things a lot," I confessed. My hands traveled along her spine.

Her eyes darkened into a stormy look of desire, and she let a little flirty pout flutter across her lips. "Should we make our way back to the house?"

That sounded better than anything in the world, except for one small thing.

I looked toward the barn, noticing the strung lights inside had flicked on.

Ian had always been great at following instructions.

"Well, whatever you have planned, I know it will be amazing." She nodded with a big grin. "And I say yes to all the chickens and goats."

"All the goats?"

Sadie nodded and winked. "All the goats and kids."

"It's time I show you something, Sadie." I stood up and slowly let her feet touch the ground.

"What are you talking about?" She slowly spun around to see a beautiful glow from the barn.

"What's going on, Zack?" She slid her hand into

mine.

"Come on. I want to show you what all I've done since last weekend."

She stood on her toes and kissed my cheek. "Okay. Lead the way."

Her small hand fit perfectly in mine as we made our way across the pasture. Sugar Beans trotted to us and walked us slowly to the barn. If I listened closely, I could hear the faint murmur of guests huddled inside. I glanced at Sadie, who slowed as she saw the white hanging lights inside.

"Zack, what's going on?" She came to a stop about ten feet from the opening of the barn.

"I love you, Sadie. That's what's going on."

Sugar Beans circled us as Sadie's eyes fastened on mine. The sun had traded for the light of the moon as my heartbeat thundered in my chest.

"Beautiful night, isn't it?" I said with my voice barely above a whisper, not wanting the magic of the night to vanish.

"It is, Zack." She licked her lips, and I desperately wanted to kiss her. "It's so good to be back home with you. I miss you when I'm gone."

I laughed. "That's a good sign."

She nodded. "I thought so."

My fingers laced with hers, and I pulled her closer. She looked into my eyes as I bent my head to kiss her again.

Everything about tonight felt mystical and like a fantasy I'd spent a lifetime conjuring.

The tenderness in her kiss edged on fiery, and I knew if I didn't stop, we'd never make it inside the barn.

I straightened, breaking our kiss, and her eyes stayed closed as she let out a little moan of satisfaction.

The evening air had cooled, but the heat between us remained fiery.

"I hope you're surprised with the progress," I said as she smiled at me.

"I'm always impressed with what you accomplish, Zack."

I knew I never wanted to beg for her love. I wanted to earn it. I wanted to be the man she deserved. The guy she'd call if her car broke down. The one she'd lean on when things got hard. When her heart hurt more than it beat, I wanted to be the man I could be proud of, and tonight, I knew I didn't need to beg for anything.

As we approached the new barn, the faint sounds of country music and muffled conversation drifted into the night air. Sadie stopped walking and looked up at me.

"What?" I asked with a curl of my lip. "I wanted to bring a little fun to your Friday night, you know. You've been studying hard."

"That's what this is all about?" she asked, raising her brows.

Damn. She was beautiful.

Her eyes brightened as we started toward the open barn door. The moment we walked inside, she gasped at the sight.

Her parents, sister, and her brother-in-law were all waving with a drink in their hands. Officer Carl gave a nod toward us while Ian took a few steps toward the stereo.

The soft light from lanterns cast playful shadows from our friends and family, who came out to support me and the love of my life.

I glanced at Sadie, and her eyes brightened with

pure excitement as she darted toward her parents. We'd only seen them once since everything had happened.

Her mom had tears in her eyes as she held her daughter close. Elena wrapped her arms around them as I walked over to her dad and stuck out my hand for a shake, which he used to pull me into a strong embrace.

He gave me a knowing look as he let go and hugged his daughter.

"This is the best surprise ever, Zack. Thank you." She grinned at me as Ian turned off the music, and she tilted her head.

"You're acting a little suspiciously," she teased. "A little jumpy, actually."

"Me? What? Who?" I feigned innocence as Ian brought over a beer for Sadie and me.

I cracked Sadie's open and did the same for myself before taking a sip.

Of all the things I'd faced in my life, I was suddenly terrified.

What if she said no?

Sadie's dad patted my back and gave me a nod of assurance.

I took another swig of beer and drew in a big breath as Ian wandered away.

Sadie caught my hand in hers, brought it to her lips, and kissed it. "You've got that look in your eyes."

I laughed. "Which one? Like I'm about to be attacked, or I'm about to attack?"

She chuckled, tracing her finger along the back of my hand. "Maybe a little of both."

I took a step toward her and took away her beer, placing both of ours on the table.

Sadie grinned. "The barn looks magical, Zack. The animals will be very grateful, very pleased."

I laughed, shaking my head. "Sadie, you make me feel so damn good."

She smiled with tears touching her lashes. "Thank you, Zack. For everything."

All eyes were on us as I pulled her into me. Our noses brushed one another before I kissed her quickly, the tension palpable.

Keeping her hand in mine, I knelt on one knee, and the crowd gasped.

Sadie brought her free hand to her mouth as I

smiled.

"Sit tight, baby. This might be a long one." I winked at her, and she chuckled. "But we've been through a lot."

"Praise be," her mom whispered.

I smiled at her parents and my brother and brought my gaze back to the love of my life.

"You are the very beat of my heart, Sadie. When I look into your eyes, I see the world how it should be. It gives me hope. You are my hope for a better future. You are my life, Sadie. My everything." I snapped my finger, and Sugar Beans came over and sat with a ring box tied to her collar. I unhooked it, and Sadie hopped on her toes a few times, trying to hide her sweet excitement.

"Sadie, I've known since the moment I met you that I wanted you to be my wife. You're a fighter, compassionate, powerful, strong, empathetic, and my very reason for living. Your dreams are mine. Your vision is our families' future. I will do everything in my power to protect you and our family. You are my world, Sadie Egorov. Will you make Sugar Beans and me the happiest man in the world? Will you marry me?"

"Zack, oh yes, baby. Your future is mine. Your dreams are my forever. I love you with all my heart, Zack Parker. You're my everything."

I slipped the ring onto her finger before she looped her arms around my neck and kissed me in a way I had never been kissed before. And I knew Sadie and Sugar Beans were my forever, and I would do everything in my power to protect her and the secrets buried deep that kept her up at night.

BOOKS BY
KARICE BOLTON

CHRISTMAS ON FIREWEED
IMAGINING LOVE ON WILLOW ROAD
CHRISTMAS CRUSH ON FIREWEED ISLAND
WAITING LOVE AT HAWTHORNE AVENUE
FOREVER CHRISTMAS ON SUGARPLUM LANE

BEYOND LOVE SERIES
BEYOND CONTROL
BEYOND DOUBT
BEYOND REASON
BEYOND INTENT
BEYOND CHANCE
BEYOND PROMISE
BEYOND the MISTLETOE

SILVER RIDGE SERIES
A HAPPY TRUTH ABOUT LOVE
A LITTLE SECRET ABOUT LOVE
A FUNNY THING ABOUT LOVE
A SURPRISING FACT ABOUT LOVE
A SIMPLE WISH ABOUT LOVE
CHRISTMAS AT SILVER RIDGE

LUKE FLETCHER SERIES
HIDDEN SINS
BURIED SINS
REDEMPTION
MIA

V MAFIA SERIES
BLAKE
DEVIN
JAXSON

SECRETS AMONG US

THE WITCH AVENUE SERIES
LONELY SOULS
ALTERED SOULS
RELEASED SOULS
SHATTERED SOULS

THE WATCHERS TRILOGY
AWAKENING
LEGIONS
CATACLYSM
TAKEN NOVELLA (A Watchers Prequel)

AFTERWORLD SERIES
RecruitZ
AlibiZ
UprisingZ

BLOOD TORN DUET
BLOOD TORN
BLOOD CURSED